Hold My Hand
& Run

Hold My Hand & Run

MARGARET McALLISTER

Dutton Children's Books

NEW YORK

CIP Data is available.

Published in the United States 2000 by Dutton Children's Books,
a division of Penguin Putnam Books for Young Readers
345 Hudson Street, New York, New York 10014
www.penguinputnam.com

Originally published in Great Britain 1999 by Oxford University Press, UK
Designed by Amy Berniker
Printed in USA   First American Edition
ISBN 0-525-46391-7
1   3   5   7   9   10   8   6   4   2

For Mum and Dad,

who first took me to the top of the cathedral tower,

and for Claire, who turned up unexpectedly

ⅯY THANKS GO TO THE FOLLOWING:

*Northumberland County Libraries, and especially the Moot Hall,
Hexham; Newcastle City Library; Roger Norris of the Dean and
Chapter Library at Durham Cathedral; Durham County Archives;
Eleanora Penman, for advice about costume; and, in particular,
to Doreen Hood and Mary Kelly, for their contribution to
Mary Fairlamb and Collywell Cross.*

Hold My Hand
& Run

ооооооооооооооо ⚜ ооооооооооооооо
C H A P T E R

Kazy Clare lay with her eyes shut, but she was wide awake, and her head was perfectly clear. She could tell, from the warmth on her face and the brightness against her eyelids, that the sun was already up on a warm summer morning. This day, she knew, was the day when she could change everything. She wondered where she and Beth would be by this time tomorrow. Where would they sleep tonight?

From the deep, snuffling breathing next to her, she knew that Beth, who had cried herself to sleep at last, would not wake yet. Little Beth had sobbed helplessly in Kazy's arms last night and had continued fretting and hiccuping while Kazy lay awake. Once she had woken screaming, but at least this time the bed was dry.

Yesterday had been a particularly bad day. There had never been a good day since Aunt Latimer arrived, but yesterday was appalling. For stammering over her lessons, Beth had been smacked and scolded. For tripping on her gown, she had been scolded, beaten, and made to stand on a stool facing the wall for an hour. And Kazy, for trying to protect her, had suffered a worse beating. All that was before the question of the fair, which had brought them both another beating with the birch rod. This time, they could hardly walk away afterward. Aunt Latimer was an elderly lady, but unusually tall and strong. She had sent them to bed hungry, too, but Joan had smuggled bread and milk to them.

In the night, questions had chased each other in Kazy's head, but only questions, not answers—how to make Father see what was happening, what could be done about Aunt Latimer, how to protect Beth from another beating? Now, in the light of a clear morning, everything was plain.

She opened her eyes, squinted at the sunlight, and winced as she sat up, because last night's cuts and bruises were stiffening. In her long, plain nightgown, she stepped on prickly rush mats to the window and looked out, past the crisscross of lead and the neat glass panes, to the towers of Cutherham Cathedral. For five hundred years, they had stood proudly against the sky. Today they were powerful guardians saying to her: It can be done, Kazy Clare. You, too, can stand strong and proud and not fall.

At thirteen she was too old for her aunt's tyranny, and Beth, who was only six, was too young. With her eyes on the cathedral towers, she made a vow.

"I, Kezia Clare of Cutherham city, solemnly swear that my sister—half sister, Elizabeth—will never be beaten again as long as I am alive to protect her. This I promise on the towers of Cutherham Cathedral and on my mother's wedding ring, on this twenty-second day of July, in the Year of Our Lord 1628." And she knew how to start.

Beth sighed in her sleep and drew her doll to her. She called it Maid Marian and loved it dearly. Kazy padded softly to the door of Aunt Latimer's bedchamber, with her heart beating so hard she could hear it.

Aunt Latimer would not tolerate creaking doors, so it was smooth and opened silently. The dark oak chest, with Aunt Latimer's initials on it, was on Kazy's left, but the keys—Aunt Latimer's household keys—were on the other side of the great curtained tent of the four-poster bed. She tiptoed very softly, listening for any change in the long drawn rhythm of Aunt Latimer's snoring.

The keys were always kept by the lady of the house. When Eliza died, Kazy had become the lady of the house, but not for long. She held her nightgown above her ankles, in case the rustling of a hem woke her aunt. The curtains were so closely drawn, it was astonishing that the old lady had not suffocated in her sleep. If she did, it would be Kazy's fault, who had wished her dead so often. She had tried to unwish it, but how could she help her first thoughts?

The keys lay beside a candle in a plain candlestick, and Kazy sank to the floor beside it. They had been happy before Aunt Latimer came, or at least they had all been safe and looked after each other. Happiness—real, careless happiness—belonged to the years when Eliza was alive, Beth's mother and Kazy's stepmother, and those years were forever. After that wretched day in January, Kazy, Beth, and Father had huddled together for comfort, sharing one another's hurts, and Kazy had done her best to fill the empty space for Beth. Then Aunt Latimer had come.

Her hand closed on the keys. The long snoring stopped, and she froze.

Aunt Latimer, sleeping, held her breath so long that Kazy feared she really had suffocated, but then there was a rattling, grunting sigh and a creak of the bed frame as she turned over. Kazy felt the sweat turn cold on her skin. But Aunt did not wake and presently snored deeply again. Kazy got up with some difficulty, owing to the keys and the long nightgown.

The keys were hers by right, and, more importantly, she would need them today. Of course, she couldn't keep these— Aunt Latimer would miss them. But there was another set, the ones Eliza had always carried, in the chest. It was just like Aunt Latimer not to use Eliza's keys.

The lock clicked, but the curtains were thick, and Aunt did not stir. Kazy lifted the lid as gently as possible, in case it creaked, just enough to slide her arm inside—but her searching fingers did not find the keys. Her hand brushed a shape that was so familiar and so thoroughly hated that her toes curled at the touch of it. It was the birch rod.

A new idea came to her, and she drew out the rod, holding it with caution and distaste as if it had a life of its own and might bite. Then, feeling in the chest again, she found the cold iron of the spare set of keys and held them tightly to keep them from rattling. If she thought for long about what she must do next, she would be too scared to do it, so she acted quickly.

The rest of the household was already waking. Joan, who did most of the work of the house, and her son, Matthew, who cared for the horses and did the heavy work, would already be up, drawing water and coaxing up a fire in the kitchen hearth. Even on hot days, water must be heated.

In the kitchen the fire was already lit, and Joan had gone out to the well. Kazy thrust the wicked birch into the fire and ran away while the twigs still crackled. She dressed quickly, resenting the need to wear black on such a day and, drawing herself up as straight and tall as she could, prepared for one more try with Father. She had tried showing him the cuts and bruises, but it hadn't helped. All he ever did was sigh and tell her that all children must expect to be beaten, but he would talk to Aunt Latimer, as if that would do any good.

The door of her father's room never did shut properly in summer, but she still knocked and, hearing no answer, peeped in. He was kneeling with closed eyes before the oak table, which served as a desk for praying, reading, and working, and his head was buried in his hands. Father was one of the cathedral canons, and the canons were among the most important clergy in Cutherham. Only the bishop and the dean were above the canons. Was that why he never had time for his family? He understood about services and how to organize the clergy and how to keep everything running smoothly at the cathedral. He surely understood about grief and loss, too, having had so much of it. He just didn't seem to understand daughters. Perhaps he was frightened of Aunt Latimer. Most people were. Kazy looked above him at the two small portraits on the wall.

In the left-hand picture was a lady with a pale face, dark eyes and eyebrows, and strong, noticeable bones. It was not a pretty face, but a handsome one, and striking, and Kazy saw something like it when she looked in a glass. It was all she knew of her own mother, the first Mistress Clare. Her name was Kezia, too. She had died giving birth to Kazy, and Kazy, who had never known her, never missed her. She wondered about her, though—but whenever she tried to ask Father about her, he changed the subject.

The other portrait still hurt when she looked at it. Eliza, her stepmother, looking as fresh and pretty as she did in life. She was Beth's mother, and Beth was like her. She was supposed to call her "Mother," but she had been used to calling her Eliza, and Eliza never minded. Eliza had carried all the brightness of a spring day with her, fair and rosy, plump like fruit in summer, breathing warmth from room to room, and no sorrow could last for long when she was there. But when that January came, and the mild, wet winter brought fever, Eliza had nursed her husband and finally fallen ill herself and had not recovered.

If you knew, thought Kazy, what has happened to bright little chatterbox Beth. She hardly dares to speak now, and when she does, she stammers. You can't help her, so I must.

"Kezia!" Her father, rising from his knees, turned and saw her and his face was all astonishment—and he never called her Kezia! Then he gave a deep, shaking sigh.

"Kazy," he said, and his voice shook, "you look so like your mother, it was as if . . . what brings you here?" He asked it as patiently as he could, but he disliked household problems, especially early in the day.

"I have to talk to you," she said, and saw the furrow of anxiety on his pale face. "Please, Father."

Most of their conversations these days began with Kazy complaining about Aunt Latimer, and Father saying that Kazy and Beth must learn to accept "little punishments," but he would "speak to their aunt." Speaking to Aunt Latimer had made no difference so far. She must be careful.

"You know we're not allowed to go to the fair this year, Father? Aunt says it's only for common people and not the right place for the cathedral families, even though we offered to do the household messages for her. Beth looked forward to it so much because Eliza used to take us every year, and we asked her again yesterday, and Aunt still said no, and Beth begged her and cried, and I begged her, too, because Beth was so upset. So Aunt thrashed us both, and Beth woke up with nightmares again."

He sighed wearily. "You must not argue with your aunt, Kazy. But perhaps a beating was harsh."

"We'd already been beaten, Father. Beth tore her gown, just a little, and it was an accident. She only tripped and . . ."

He frowned and looked over her head. "I will have a word with your aunt."

". . . and in the morning, she was struggling with her lessons," Kazy hurried on, trying harder, "and Aunt took the hornbook and hit her over the head. I'm not saying we should never be punished, but Aunt does it all the time." But already he was collecting books together, ready to go to the cathedral or the deanery. Kazy placed herself between her father and the door. "Don't you ever look at Beth? She's always quiet, she stammers. She never used to be clumsy, but now she's so frightened she drops things and trips over her gowns. She's not allowed to help Matthew with the horses or Joan in the kitchen, and she loved that. She's not even allowed to play with the cats, and you won't notice, you won't even look at her because . . ."

She stopped suddenly. She had gone too far. They both knew why he would not look at Beth. Beth was unbearably like Eliza. The face her father turned to her was pale with grief and anger, but she had his attention at last.

It was too late. A door banged, and heavy skirts swished along the floor. A voice, harsh and rasping as a gull's cry, rang out, and Kazy's stomach tightened.

"Walter! Walter, I must speak to you! At once!" Aunt Latimer stood in the doorway, grim-faced, tall, and simmering with anger. In her heavy black gown with her lined, angry face above a stiff and yellowing ruff, she looked like a messenger of death. Kazy curtsied, but she looked defiantly into Aunt's eyes before she left the room and slipped behind the door to listen, as she always did these days. She needed to know if there was trouble brewing, so she could keep Beth out of it.

"Walter, the birch rod is missing," announced Aunt Latimer severely. "I put it in the chest last night and there is now no trace of it."

"I am sure," he replied patiently, "you can have no need of the birch rod at this hour in the morning."

"That is not important. It is missing, Walter. I know I left it there."

"Frances, you had such a headache last night. You told me of it. You know you forget things when your headaches are very bad. I'm sure you have misplaced it. I shall ask Joan to search."

"Joan," said Aunt sourly, "may know all too well where to find it. She spoils the children as badly as your wife ever did."

Kazy turned hot, then cold. She had not imagined that suspicion would fall on Joan.

"Or Kezia," said Aunt. "Kezia could have taken it. Walter, you have no idea what that child is capable of. She opposes me in everything. The birch rod is not sufficient for her. I need a whip."

"Frances, I forbid that!" Kazy jerked in surprise. Father had never stood up to Aunt before.

"Forbid!" Aunt's voice grew more than ever like the cry of a gull. "I give your daughters the firmness they need, and you forbid it! Your wife should have chastised them more!"

"She did not need to," he said, "and the dean must not be kept waiting."

Kazy had begun to hope. Now hope turned gray and disappeared. As usual, her father was running away, going to see the dean, putting off the need to resist Aunt Latimer. Forbidding her to use a whip was one thing. Preventing her was another, and Kazy feared the worst.

"I will be home late, Frances," continued Canon Clare. Kazy could imagine him avoiding his sister's eyes. "If the birch rod has not presented itself, we will speak further on the matter."

You'll be too late, she thought, and went to help Beth dress.

Kazy had done her best to look after Beth and Father after Eliza died, and, of course, there was Joan. But Aunt Latimer, who was Father's sister and a widow, had decided that she was needed to run the household, and, on a stormy April day, she had moved in. Soon after, there had been a day of such heartlessness that it still hurt Kazy to remember it. "You are too old for toys, Kezia! Beth, what do you want with such tawdry things!" And Aunt had taken the little wooden horse Kazy had kept since she was a baby and tossed it onto the blazing kitchen fire. The string of painted beads Beth called her jewels had followed. The sight of the shriveling remains in the fireplace had left them both sobbing loudly in Joan's apron, then trying to cry more quietly when they were beaten for it, but when tears were dried, Kazy had made sure it would not happen again. Joan had helped her sew secret pockets into gowns and petticoats, where the overflowing gathers kept them hidden. They had often been useful, those pockets. Joan had never missed a chance to slip in a penny or an apple or bread and meat if Aunt had sent them to bed hungry. There were more important treasures in the little oak box in the girls' bedchamber, but it could only be a matter of time before Aunt found out about those.

"Kezia, Kezia, your house is on fire!" In the old days Beth used to sing that little rhyme first thing in the mornings, because she thought it was so witty, and because it annoyed

Kazy. But now, when Kazy woke her, she squeaked a little with pain from yesterday's beating, felt the bed, and dressed with no more than a whisper. She was still rosy from sleep, but the face under the yellow curls was solemn, and the large blue eyes were wary all the time.

Magdalen's Day Fair was a great event in Cutherham. Such throngs packed together that it was said to be a breeding ground for fevers in the hot weather, but, all the same, most of Cutherham went. Kazy, looking out of the parlor window that sunny morning, saw them streaming through the streets, hopeful children, servants and apprentices given the day off, merchants' wives, and old grandmothers. Some were hoping for bargains, and others went to sneer at the ribbons and cloths at the fair and say loudly that the shops in Cutherham sold far better. Some went to consult the tooth-puller or the sellers of potions. But most went because everyone else went, and this was the real joy of the fair—to meet old friends and relations, to catch up on gossip, and to have a summer holiday. This day was a day of burning sunshine. The Clare sisters, locked in the parlor of the Cutherham house, watched from the windows.

"I w-wi-wish we could go out," whispered Beth.

"We will," said Kazy.

There were a few who did not go to the fair. Mistress Latimer had few friends and was above such things as fairs. She had tried to make Kezia and Beth understand that a canon's daughters should not go to common entertainments, but Beth had only cried and Kezia, as usual, had been insolent. It was

Walter's fault, for marrying a common servant girl. At least Kezia's mother had been a lady. You only had to look at Beth to know she was a peasant's brat. She had agreed, grudgingly, to Joan and Matthew going to the fair, but Kazy and Beth remained at home with the doors locked.

And the birch rod was missing. She suspected Kezia, but was not quite sure—not perfectly sure—that she had put it in the chest. And there was something else strange about that chest, something else missing, if she could only remember what. In the afternoon she made her way down the winding streets to the apothecary's shop. The hot weather gave her unbearable headaches, and she would not buy medicine from the frauds at the fair.

"W-wh-wha-what are you doing, Kazy?" Beth struggled with the words as Kazy came from the kitchen.

"I'm getting you some apples. Put them in your secret pockets."

Beth shrank away in surprise and fear. Kazy wrapped bread, cheese, cold meat, and more apples in a napkin, pressed them into a basket, and folded a kerchief over the top.

"W-w-w . . . " Beth stopped, and tried again. "W" was her hardest sound. "We'll be beaten," she whispered.

"No." Kazy pushed a parcel of Joan's gingerbread down the side of the basket. It had been made for Beth and herself, so they might as well have it. "Stay there, Beth. I need some things from upstairs."

She had a little money of her own, her precious recorders, and her own mother's jewelry—a small necklace of pearls, the earrings to wear with it, and her wedding ring. It was not simply for love of them that she tucked them into her concealed pocket, but because they might be needed. She took the letter she had already written, with a lot of alterations, and folded two cloaks, although they were heavy, and it seemed absurd to take them on such a day. It was a shame her lute and the virginals would have to stay behind, when she loved her music so much. She could play just once more, now, just for a minute . . . no. No! Aunt might be back soon. She carried her belongings to the parlor.

"Now, Bethy," she said briskly, "time to go. I have the spare keys."

Beth stared helplessly, the way she did when Aunt Latimer reached for the rod.

"No, w-w-we'll be . . ."

Kazy took both her hands and held them tightly. "She's never, ever going to birch you again. We're going to find some people who'll look after you."

"Can M-Mai-Maid Marian come?"

"She's in the basket. Quickly, now, before Aunt comes back."

"W-wha-what about Father?"

"I've written him a letter."

Kazy ran up the stairs and placed her letter on her father's desk, but it was hard to leave it there. She felt it tugging at her like a child, urging her to stay at home, to change her mind and sleep in her own bed tonight. If she thought of her father she would certainly stay, so instead she thought of Beth, the beatings and the burned treasures and all the times they had been deprived of food and music and the fresh summer air. She thought of the way Beth used to sing and chatter and hide behind doors ready to jump out, and of Beth now, stammering and clumsy, waking to fear every morning.

She left the letter on the desk, and it was the hardest thing she had ever done.

On the far side of the city, the fair-day crowds sweated in the sun and thought of the journey home. Kazy and Beth slipped out over Bishopsgate Bridge, with a last look back at the cathedral. It made Kazy feel strong.

She had decided, as she made her plans that morning, that Willowsford seemed the best place to go. Eliza's brother and his family lived there. Kazy had never been to Willowsford, but she knew it was north of Cutherham. The road north lay over Bishopsgate Bridge and presently divided into two—the main road east to the crowded, busy town of Highbridge-on-Tarl, and the narrower, winding road west, to Abbey St. Andrew. Willowsford was on the west road, which, Kazy reasoned, would be safer. It was quiet, and they were less likely to be noticed.

Sweat prickled the back of her neck and made her dress scratchy. Her basket and the two cloaks were heavy, and she resented the long sleeves and heavy skirt of what was meant to be a gown for all seasons. The small leather bottle she had brought held very little ale for two of them on a day of such glaring heat, but sooner or later, she supposed, they would find a stream. Beth padded trustfully beside her.

"Wh-whe-where are we going?"

"Willowsford," said Kazy. Their father had relations in York and her own mother's family lived there, too—but it was no good running to them. None of them had approved of Father marrying Eliza, so they would hardly care for Eliza's child. They'd probably only send them straight home again. "You have an uncle and aunt at Willowsford."

"I do? Have I met them?"

"No, but your mother had a brother named Edward Sheppard. Uncle and Aunt Sheppard live at Willowsford. We'll go to them, and you'll meet your cousins."

At least it was somewhere to head for, and, if they were lucky, Uncle and Aunt Sheppard would let them stay. Kazy could make herself useful and even Beth, she supposed, could help with the poultry. So they walked and walked, and the sun was hot and the basket was heavy, and the little sips from the bottle had left it almost empty. It was a slow journey, for they had to walk at Beth's pace, and though Kazy pointed out flowers and animals, Beth hardly ever spoke except to ask how far it was to Willowsford and were they nearly there yet.

Kazy rubbed her face. The rough, stony road wound on between fields, past farmhouses, and out of sight. She had no idea how far they had come.

"Not yet," she said. "Come on now, Beth."

She took a tiny sip from the bottle, but she was so thirsty by now that it made no difference. Her throat was so dry it hurt her to speak. "Finish the rest of that, Beth. We'll call at the next house we see and ask for a drink."

The road felt rough through their shoes, and their gowns were growing dusty at the hems, but there was a light breeze. When Beth saw a calf, with enormous dark eyes in its gentle young face, she stopped to watch it and half smiled. Birds sang, and wild fragrant honeysuckle tangled in the hedges, and a colt in a field bounded and kicked for joy of freedom, and . . .

"Listen!" said Kazy. There was a splash of water on stones. On their right, they saw a gently wooded slope, which gave way to a stream giggling over pebbles. Stumbling and holding hands to keep each other from slipping, they scrambled down the bank, and Beth, holding up her skirt, waddled toward the shallows.

"Hey! Don't you drink that!"

Two women, red-faced in the heat, stood at a little distance with yokes and leather pails at their feet. From the shady, wooded rocks above them, a spring splashed down, and one of the women was holding a pail underneath it.

"You're not to drink that!" called the first woman, who was small and round and was ambling toward them. "D'you not know better?"

Beth, up to her ankles in the stream, stood still and looked as if she wanted to disappear. Kazy stopped with the toe of one shoe in the water.

"That's a bad stream in this weather," said the woman,

clambering down the path. "Has no one told you? In the heat and the dry spells it's not for drinking. There was many took bad with it last year."

"Come out, Beth," ordered Kazy.

"I doubt it'll do her any harm, just plodging about in it," said the woman. "But you don't want it on the insides of you. You never know what's died in it, upstream."

"Never mind, pet," said the other woman, who was still patiently filling buckets at the spring. "This water comes through the rock. It never fails us."

Kazy and Beth scrambled gratefully up the hill and drank from their hands, splashing their hot faces. The water was icy cold and tingled.

"Aye, it's cold from the rock," said the second woman. "That's good water." She watched as they drank and splashed. "You're not from here, are you? Are you from Cutherham?"

"Yes, we're on our way back there," said Kazy, who had just decided to lay as many false trails as possible. "We've been visiting our aunt in Willowsford."

"Willowsford! But that's two days' journey! Three, I should think, with the little one! She can't possibly have walked it!"

Kazy's spirits sank, and she tried not to show it. "We had a ride in a cart," she said.

"Now mind," said the first woman, "don't you drink the water in Cutherham. Cities are filthy places."

Kazy waited until they were well out of sight, then she took Beth's hand and continued along the Willowsford road.

"How far is it to Willowsford now?" asked Beth. She was dragging her feet, and the sun was in her eyes.

Mistress Latimer leaned against the doorpost in the dark house in Cutherham and panted for breath. Her face was red and perspiring and her eyes furious. The unnatural silence in the house told her the thing she had dreaded.

They had not come back.

She had arrived home that afternoon to a silent absence of children. She had searched the house, the stable, and the kitchen garden before taking up the poker—the best weapon available—and striding through the streets, unaware that the crowds coming home from the fair were turning their heads to look at the ridiculous grim-faced woman. Yet, for all her efforts, she had not found them. Heavily, she dropped the poker and dragged her way upstairs.

Walter Clare sat at his desk. His head was lowered in his hands and turned from side to side as if he were saying no, no, to the paper lying in front of him. He looked up with no tears on his face, but his color was gray, as if he had grown old in an afternoon.

"They are gone," he said bleakly. "Kazy has written a letter."

The bundle of hay was new and sweet smelling. Kazy lay on her side with her arms full of Beth and watched the slowly changing sky of the summer night. It was growing cooler, and she snuggled the cloaks and hay more closely around them.

Willowsford was farther than she had thought, but another good day's walking might get them there. The food would soon run out, but she had a little money, and maybe a farm would sell them bread. In Cutherham there had been a girl and two men who played music in the street for money, and she had her recorders with her.

Beth was safe, and that was the most important thing. Then Kazy remembered the two women at the spring and how Beth had come so close to drinking that water. A shadowy feeling came over her, and she touched Beth's forehead to make quite sure she was not ill. Beth was always catching coughs, sometimes quite bad coughs, and she wasn't sure where she could get the medicines for a cough.

Walter Clare and his sister came downstairs to find Joan red-eyed and tight-lipped. When she saw them she turned her back and marched to the kitchen, where she could be heard angrily banging the pots about. Matthew, stacking logs in the hearth, stood up with respect.

"At first light, Matthew," said Canon Clare, "ride to Highbridge. Here is money for your journey, and your mother will give you food and drink. If, on the way, you see my daughters, you are to bring them home. If anyone asks any questions concerning them, they are staying with Mistress Lawrence. That is all."

Matthew gave something between a nod and a bow and left. It was all very well to say "bring them home." What if they didn't want to come?

"I will ride to York myself," Canon Clare went on, "and

send someone to Abbey St. Andrew. Go to bed, Frances. We have nothing to say to one another tonight."

But Canon Clare did not go to bed, not for a long time. He sat up and wondered where his daughters would spend the night and whether they were cold and hungry and lost.

Both his daughters resembled their mothers. Kezia had been determined, talented, and strong willed, and so was Kazy. Perhaps he had forgotten that Kazy was only thirteen and had lost the only mother she had ever known. And Beth—he would give everything, now, to see Beth looking at him with Eliza's blue eyes. Since Eliza died he had lived every moment in grief. Nothing could be worse, until now.

The rising sun in her face woke Kazy early. Stalks of hay prickled her back, and her shoulders were stiff. She shuffled and looked down at Beth, who, tired out, had slept without nightmares.

"Lazy Lizzy! I know you're awake."

Beth did not move, but when Kazy tickled her she squirmed and sat up, her hair untidy and her cheeks pink. They stood up and shook bits of stalk out of dresses, which felt unnaturally cramped and uncomfortable and a touch damp. Kazy hadn't thought of bringing a comb, but Beth produced one from her secret pocket.

"It was M-M-Mother's," said Beth. "And I didn't w-wa-want Aunt Latimer to . . ."

"Yes, I know," said Kazy. "The sooner we get to Willowsford, the better."

After a small breakfast—there was not much food for a

long journey—they followed the course of the stream as closely as possible. There was less chance that way of anyone seeing them from the road, and Kazy hoped to find another spring.

"I think, Beth," she said, "in case Aunt Latimer sends anyone to search for us, we should use different names in front of other people. Nobody must know who we really are. If we meet anyone you must pretend I'm called . . ." She had always liked "Beatrice," but Beth would never remember that. "Kate. It's very like Kazy. What do you call me?"

"K-K-Kate. Katie, Kate, Kate," chanted Beth. "And I'm M-M-Marian, like Maid Marian. Look, Kazy—Kate, look at that cow. Is that w-w-why we mustn't drink the w-water?"

Ahead of them, on the other bank, stood a cow, its feet splayed, adding to the volume of the stream. Having finished by adding a steaming heap to the water, it tried to clamber up the sides of the bank, but it was too large and clumsy. It slithered, lowed miserably, gave up, and stood in the river as if waiting to be rescued.

"Can we help?"

Kazy had been wondering this, too, but she had no experience with cows.

"I don't see how. We can't get it up that bank, and if we did, we don't know where it belongs, so we might get it even more lost than it already is. Someone will come looking for the silly thing."

After a long walk and a lot of explaining to Beth about why they couldn't milk the cow because you need a stool or something and a bucket, and besides they might get kicked, they came to a place where the stream was shallow, and a stretch of sand and pebbles opened out. Sunlight through the trees dappled onto the water, and a spring gurgled from the rock. They drank eagerly and splashed their faces.

"I could do with a wash, to cool down," said Kazy, struggling with the lacings at her back. "Help me off with my gown and petticoat, Beth."

"You can't!" exclaimed Beth as Kazy, in only her white smock, picked her way down the pebbly shore. "If-if-if someone comes?"

"I'll go out of sight, then, beyond the trees," she said. She folded her gown and petticoat, with their precious pockets, and carefully pushed them between two boulders beside Beth. "And I'll take my cloak in case anyone does come, Mistress Modesty. Stay here, Beth, and don't move from this spot. If anyone comes, or if you're frightened, call me. What should you call me?"

"K-Kate."

Kazy carried her cloak and put her shoes back on to hobble over the pebbly shore. In the shallows there was a pool where she splashed cold water on her arms and neck, getting her hair wet. With her shoes off, the water felt fresh and delicious on her tired feet. Little sprigs of grass and hay floated away as she flexed her toes.

"Ka-Kate! Kate!" It was a wail of distress. Kazy pushed her wet feet into her shoes, snatched up the cloak, and ran as well as she could.

She saw them before they saw her. There were two scruffy young men in farm laborer's smocks and breeches. One—

dark, gangly, and pimply—was holding Maid Marian high above Beth's reach while the other laughed. His foot was almost touching Kazy's folded gown.

"What a temper!" The tall one laughed as Beth screamed, kicked, and grasped for her doll. "We only came looking for a cow, and look what we've found!"

The other, who was ginger-haired and stocky, stepped forward, caught his toe on Kazy's gown, and looked down to see what had obstructed him. Kazy pulled her cloak around her with one hand, stretched out the other, and thought of her aunt.

"Stop, you filth!" she cried in her best Aunt Latimer voice. "Leave that child! Touch nothing, or . . ."

They stopped, startled, but not frightened.

"Or what?" asked the gingery one, grinning stupidly. Kazy thought quickly.

"Or I'll make you wish you never saw the sun rise!"

The dark one dropped the doll. Beth snatched it up and hugged it.

"And who do you think you are?" asked the other, but he looked less swaggering than before. Kazy had no idea what a striking figure she made, standing at a distance with her dark hair wet and straggled about, the cloak flung wildly over her smock, the wet skin of her outstretched arm gleaming and her eyes glaring under the dark eyebrows. She saw the admiration on Beth's face, though, and was inspired.

"If you leave us now, and tell no one that you have seen us, you will find your cow two miles upstream, safe and well. But do any harm against us or tell a living soul that you have seen us, and I will lay down a curse that will make your beasts swell and burst, and you yourselves shall run mad."

"We're going," said the tall one, backing away. "Come on, Rob." But Rob was harder to shake.

"She's a fraud," he said. "She's just a lass. What's she so anxious to hide? What's in here?"

To Kazy's terror and fury, he squatted down and reached for the folded gown. She pointed her finger at him, and began to chant.

"*Luo, luo. Lueis, luei, luomen, luete . . .*"

"Spare us, we're going! We're sorry! Leave us alone! PLEASE!" Pleading and stumbling over the stones, they ran, and Kazy gathered Beth in her arms.

"Did they hurt you, Bethy? Did they take anything? God forgive me, I'll never leave you alone again!"

But Beth was gazing at her with shining eyes.

"Kazy! How did you do that?"

"It was all I could think of. It's a Greek verb."

"I wi-wi-wish I could learn Greek. Father forgets my lessons."

"I know. He forgets mine, too. I hope I got the verb right. We'll stay by the road from now on, just in case they change their minds and come back."

"My feet hurt," said Beth as they trudged along. "Is W-W-Willowsford far?"

"I don't know," said Kazy, trying to be patient. Once they had heard a cart in the distance, but fearing that the farm lads might be on it, she had hidden Beth and herself behind the bushes. But the road was long and hard, and the day was hot and dry, and neither showed any sign of changing. When a rumbling of wheels and a clip of hooves sounded behind them, Kazy steered Beth toward the shelter of the trees.

"Stay here with me," she said. "You may as well sit down for a minute."

Beth flopped heavily, sighed, and pulled up a bit of fern to fan herself with. Kazy watched and listened from behind a tree.

The cart sounded smoother than farm carts. As it came into sight, she saw it was brightly painted.

"Beth," called Kazy, "you can come out! It's all right! It's people from the fair!"

She stood by the road, waving, as the cart slowed down.

"Can we ride with you?" she called. "We're on our way to Willowsford!"

Walter Clare sat at one side of the darkly gleaming table with his old friend, Canon Hunt, on the other. Kazy's letter lay between them.

"If Eliza had lived . . ." said Canon Clare.

"Exactly so," said Canon Hunt. "But Eliza is dead."

It seemed that everything depended on Eliza Clare, even now that she had been dead for seven months.

Walter Clare had been a well-known scholar. Many years ago he had taught young men at Oxford, but he had been noticed by Bishop Patterson, who made sure that Walter became the youngest canon at Cutherham Cathedral. Bishop Patterson's brilliant young daughter had noticed him, too, and he had arrived in Cutherham as a young clergyman with an excellent brain, a compassionate heart, and a young wife. Kezia Clare was a striking girl with dark determined looks and a firm, quick step. She was related to the best families in three counties and was said to be as well educated as her husband. Within a year she had died in childbirth, leaving a daughter, also named Kezia—but Canon Clare, though he loved her dearly, called her Kazy, because he could not quite bear to call her Kezia. Kezia's sister, the wealthy Mistress Katherine Lawrence of York, offered to take the child into her family, but Canon Clare would not part with Kazy, who was spoiled and fussed over by servants and neighbors.

As a lonely widower, he was often at the home of his friend Canon Nicholas Hunt, where he and Kazy were always welcome. There was a large family there, including Hunt's elderly mother, and, when little Kazy was five years old, a new servant arrived to look after old Mrs. Hunt.

Her name was Eliza Sheppard, and she came from a farming family in Willowsford. She was a rounded, fair-haired, sensible girl, with a kind heart. She could hardly read and write at all, but she could make a room welcoming, soothe hurt feelings, nurse any ailment, make perfect custards, and practice firm kindness even with stubborn little Kazy Clare. Above all else, she could make Walter Clare happy.

When Walter announced that he and Eliza were to be married, his sister, Frances Latimer, was disgusted. The idea of an ignorant servant marrying into the family so horrified her that she declared she would never speak to him again, nor meet his wife. Katherine Lawrence was worried, too. She wrote again, imploring him to "send little Kezia to my keeping, for I shall love her as mine own, and she will be brought up as fitting her mother's memory." But Walter, Eliza, and Kazy stayed happily together and, in 1621, Beth was born.

Canon Hunt thanked God daily for that bright, happy family, but he wished he could change what had happened on the last day of 1627. That was the day when he and Walter Clare took alms to the poor of Cutherham. In one of those wretched homes, Canon Clare had caught the fever that nearly killed him. Eliza had nursed him herself, staying beside him night and day, never letting the children near in case they caught the infection. No one did catch it except Eliza herself, who died insisting that the children were not brought to see her.

He folded his hands, rubbed his thumbs together, and looked across the table.

"You think, Walter, that they may have gone to York?"

"Yes, to Katherine," said Walter. "Or to Highbridge, being nearer. Or, God forbid, to London. I have sent messengers."

"Try Abbey St. Andrew," suggested Canon Hunt, "or Willowsford. Eliza's brother is there."

"Edward Sheppard, yes," said Canon Clare. "But they have never met him, even though he often comes to Cutherham market. He is a proud man who works on the land and does not want to take advantage of Eliza's marriage. He keeps his distance. Kazy would not go there. She wrote in her letter that she would write to me again. But she will not return to my house until . . ." He picked up the letter and read, " '. . . until there is no tyrant to rule over me. For Beth must not be so cruelly used, and nor should I.' Since Eliza died," he went on, "Kazy has done everything for love of Beth. Perhaps I forgot how young she was."

Kazy sat beside the driver of the cart, swinging her legs and enjoying the light breeze. Beth, who had turned shy and silent again, sat on the other side. The man between them, so tall, thin, and scraggily bearded that he reminded Kazy of a bare tree, said little, but occasionally gave a small, kind smile in Beth's direction. Behind them in the cart sat the most enormous woman Kazy had ever seen. She wore a faded blue gown with a tattered hem, a pink kerchief around her shoulders, and a great quantity of necklaces. The man called her Ma, but Kazy doubted she could be his mother.

"What you running away from, then?" asked Ma over her shoulder.

"We're not running away," said Kazy. "We're visiting our aunt in—"

"Willowsford, yes, you said so," said Ma. "Have it your own way, then. We'll leave you at Willowsford, then go on to Little Wennbridge. We'll sell a few bits. Sell a bit at Willowsford, too." She helped herself to a dark, juicy plum from a basket, handed another two to the girls, and ate noisily.

"Where else will you go?" asked Kazy.

"Round the villages and out to the farms, anywhere we can sell a bit. They don't get much to the fairs, out from them places with the roads so bad, so we bring the fairs to them. Do a bit of work on the land, if it's offered, and settle in Highbridge for the winter. We can buy cloth and trinkets cheap at Cutherham fair and get a good price at Highbridge."

"About enough to keep us out of the lockup," said the tinker.

"And when, may I ask, did you ever see the inside of a lockup?" Ma wriggled her enormous bottom with indignation.

"The fact is, there's a many places we can't go these days. Play a bit of music, sell a few ribbons, and the next thing you know you're turned out and moved on for vagrancy—or, what's far worse, whipped."

"So it's against the law to play music for money?" asked Kazy, who had hoped to do exactly that.

"As I say, it depends on where you are. Round here, these little places, no one would bother you. Wouldn't pay much, though, if you thought to try it."

"Oh, no, I wasn't going to . . ."

" 'Course you wasn't, 'course you wasn't. But if you was, you'd not make a living at it, not round here." She laughed loudly at Beth, who was licking stickiness from her hand. "What a state, lassie! That's right, lick your little hand clean—God in heaven, who's done this?"

She had caught sight of Beth's palm and pulled it toward her to get a better look. It was crisscrossed with thin lines, some faded, some still clear. Beth squirmed and hid her fist in the folds of her gown.

"Her back is far worse," said Kazy. "And her legs. And mine. That's why we're going to Willowsford."

"Well, if anyone asks, *I* haven't seen you two," said Ma. "But there's no money in the music these days. At one time tinkers could do charms and that, but not now. The least whiff of witchcraft and the law comes down on you."

Kazy said nothing, but she and Beth glanced at each other and then away, quickly. There was an uncomfortable silence until Ma pointed to a row of ramshackle houses around a strip of grass and said, "That's Willowsford."

"W-wha-what are they staring at?" whispered Beth, pressing close to Kazy.

"The cart, I think," said Kazy.

By the time the cart stopped a crowd was waiting, for a visit from the tinkers was a rare treat. There were plenty of people to direct them to the Sheppard house, and Kazy stopped to make Beth tidy and pick grass out of her hair. It was too late now to think that they might not be welcome, that Aunt Sheppard might be no better than Aunt Latimer, that there might be too many mouths to feed already. She led the way to the house, which was long and low, with a coarse thatch of heather. "Hens!" said Beth as the fowls scratched in the yard around them. Two small, dirty children sat on a fence, swinging their bare legs, and a woman came out of the farmhouse rubbing her hands on her apron. She was thin with a lined, worried face and seemed much older than Eliza ever did, but she looked as if she'd know what to do.

"Mistress Sheppard?" said Kazy. "I'm Canon Clare's daughter, Kazy. I've brought Eliza's daughter to you. This is Beth."

The woman dropped to her knees and ran her roughened hand very gently over Beth's curls as Beth shrank back against Kazy.

"Annie! Joseph!" she called. "Run and fetch your father!"

There was a lot of explaining to be done, but it was done over a plain supper that evening. Kazy had expected Uncle Sheppard to be like an older, male version of Eliza. She had not expected a man hardened by years of exhausting work in harsh weather. He walked with a limp, and there was always a furrow of pain on his forehead. When the rough bread and broth supper was over and the long table in the dark, smoke-smelling room was cleared, the smaller children disappeared to play with the cats under the table and Kazy faced her uncle. Aunt Sheppard and the two older boys—Eddie, who was almost grown up, and Will, who was about her own age—stayed with them. Uncle Sheppard leaned his elbows on the table.

"So you're telling me," he said, "that you've just up and left your father, and you think you can turn up here and we'll take your part?"

"I'll write to him and tell him where we are. But we're not going home while Aunt Latimer's allowed to beat Beth."

"If you were my daughters, I'd give you a hiding," he growled, but Aunt Sheppard intervened.

"It's not just a question of hidings, Edward, they're all black and blue and scarred. That Latimer woman's not a fit person to care for them."

"Well, they can't stay here, whatever else."

Kazy had already realized that there was scarcely room for the family in the house. Everyone wore old, worn clothes, and the children had outgrown theirs. And would there be enough to eat in winter? Even one more child would be too much.

"They can't go back to that woman," repeated Aunt Sheppard. "Kazy was right to bring Eliza's lass to us. Tell you what we'll do, Kazy. Your uncle's going to Cutherham market this week. He can call on your father, to say you're safe. We'll sort something out. Now, look at that bairn!"

Beth, yawning enormously, had climbed into Kazy's lap and was nestling in with her thumb in her mouth. Uncle Sheppard's long face relaxed, and he smiled.

"She's like our Eliza at the same age," he said, "and for Eliza's sake, I'd gladly have her. But you can't just run off and turn up here like this. Times have been bad. It was a rough winter, and since our Eliza . . ." He paused, but his wife went on.

"Eliza used to visit us every year, did you know? She always brought something for the children—clothes and such—she helped. She helped our Will to get his apprenticeship."

Will looked up and grinned. He had rough fair hair and a pleasant, open face.

"I'm going to Abbey St. Andrew," he said. "To be apprenticed to a cabinetmaker."

"Eliza arranged that," said Aunt Sheppard, "along with the people at Collywell Cross, where she used to work before she went to Cutherham. She paid to have our Will apprenticed."

"That's enough for tonight," said Uncle Sheppard. "The bairns are ready to sleep. I'll see your father, and we'll soon have you home."

Home? Kazy wondered if he had understood anything at all. She placed Beth in Aunt Sheppard's arms and stood up.

"Uncle Sheppard," she said, "if I have to go home—if I absolutely have to—I will. But all the reason for bringing Beth here is to protect her, and she is not to go back!"

Her uncle's face grew grim. A vein in his forehead stood

out, blue under the skin. He rose to his feet and seemed much bigger than before.

"Now, young madam," he said with quiet anger, "that may be the way you speak to your father, but you needn't do it here. Not unless you want a right good birching such as your aunt never gave you!"

She was ready to answer, but a voice interrupted her. It was a stammering, frightened voice, making a valiant effort.

"You m-mu-mustn't beat my sister! Your b-be-beasts will burst, and . . ." she was running out of courage, and her voice faltered, ". . . and you'll go m-mad." And she added in a shy whisper, "From the curses." Scared by her own boldness, she put her thumb back in her mouth and hid her face.

Silence hung like the pause between lightning and thunder. Uncle Sheppard took a step back. Aunt Sheppard slipped Beth from her lap, held her at arm's length, and looked fearfully into her face.

"God in heaven, it's witchcraft," said Uncle Sheppard at last. "And from a clergyman's daughters!"

"It's not possible," said Aunt Sheppard, but she still held Beth away from her. "You didn't mean such wicked things, did you, Beth?" But Beth was too afraid to speak again.

"Of course it's not possible," said Kazy quickly. "It's just something I said. I pretended to be a witch to scare away some boys who were going to steal from us. I had to do something at once, and that was all I could think of. I said a bit of Greek."

"God have mercy, she knows Greek!" muttered her uncle,

as if it were worse than witchcraft. So Kazy told them exactly what had happened.

"That's what comes of giving a girl a schooling," said Uncle Sheppard. "Greek! So now, if them lads tell anyone about it, you could be arrested for witchcraft. And you're under our roof."

"And they'll stay under it, for this night at least," said Aunt Sheppard. "Perhaps the lads didn't tell, and if they did, who would search here? Now you can all settle down for the night."

The children all slept in that one large room on the floor. It was hard, but warmer and drier than a haystack. As she was drifting off to sleep, Kazy heard Will whispering to her.

"Kazy? You awake?"

"No."

"What will you do? If you can't stay here, and you won't go home?"

"I'll find somewhere. Somewhere safe for Beth."

"There's Collywell Cross. I think it's near Abbey St. Andrew. Well, not near, but sort of near . . ."

"Hold your noise and get to sleep," said a voice.

"Tell you in the morning," said Will.

At their very early breakfast, Kazy, rubbing her eyes and finding it hard to be awake, couldn't see Will anywhere.

"He's away with your uncle," said her aunt. "To Cutherham." She stood up and swept crumbs from the table. "It's Cutherham market tomorrow. Beth!"

She filled Beth's hands with scraps for the hens and

watched her trot out to the yard. Aunt Sheppard never stopped working as she went on talking to Kazy. "Your father has to be told, lass, he has to know where you are."

Beth, running back in, tripped over the step and fell sprawling on the floor. She was on her feet again instantly and peering at the front of her gown. It had picked up nothing but a few dust marks, but she darted like a frightened animal to Kazy's lap, where she hid her head.

"All's safe here, Beth. Nobody here will beat you just for falling over," said Kazy, stroking Beth's curls. She looked up at her aunt. "Beth was never clumsy before Aunt Latimer came. It's just because she's frightened."

Aunt Sheppard looked at Beth as if she were a strange-looking kitten that had wandered in, but presently she took her hand and sent her off with one of her own children to help with the hay. "Mind, but she's just to fetch and carry," she said. "Don't let her near them sharp scythes. Kazy, can you bake?"

Kazy had helped with the bread baking before, as both her stepmother and Joan believed that any woman should know how to feed a household, whatever her social standing. It was different in the farm kitchen, though, where the flour was coarser and grainier than anything Kazy was used to.

"Now," said her aunt as they worked, "your uncle and your father will sort things out with your aunt, then you can go home."

Kazy couldn't imagine it being that easy. "If that doesn't work," she said, "Beth likes it here."

"Maybe she does, but she can't stay. I'm sorry, lass, but

you've seen the way things are. Bairns are the one thing we have enough of. Besides, you and Beth are gentlewomen, not country lasses. Mind you don't get that dough too wet."

"She's never to touch Beth again," said Kazy, and rammed her fists into the dough.

Over the following days Kazy learned more of the work of the kitchen than she had ever learned in her life, and she helped to milk and to churn butter. Beth helped, too, when she wasn't in the fields with the haymakers. The wary look left her eyes, and she began to laugh with the other children. But when the farm children grew excited and began running up the road at every opportunity to see if their father and Will were coming home, Kazy, scrubbing the dairy, grew anxious and distracted, until her aunt said, "For mercy's sake, take your sister and go up to the haymaking. You're as twitchy as a cat in thunder."

Kazy took off her apron to go up to the fields, but the sound of running footsteps made her stop. Will burst into the room, red-faced and sweating.

"For the love of God, she's a madwoman! Mother, get the lasses out of the way! I ran ahead to warn you!"

A familiar voice rang from the farmyard. After a few days of freedom, it was all the more terrifying.

"Teach me no lessons, sir! I shall take this into my own hands!"

Beth was already rigid with terror. Kazy looked for the door that led to the newly scrubbed dairy, bundled Beth through it, followed her, and ran for the fields. When, seconds later, Aunt Latimer stormed into the house, dark with rage and carrying a whip, she saw only Will with his back to the window and Aunt Sheppard looking puzzled. Uncle Sheppard came behind her, silently shaking his head.

Staying out of sight of the house, Kazy led Beth to the far side of the sloping field where the hay lay drying. They lay among grass and cornstalks.

"She w-w-won't find us, will she?" whispered Beth.

"No, but keep quiet."

Kazy strained her ears. Aunt Latimer had a loud voice and didn't realize how far it carried. It was impossible to make out words, but the noise of shouting and banging on the table was so clear that a crowd of interested neighbors had gathered outside the house. Entertainment as good as this was rare in Willowsford.

Then another voice was raised, a high, clear voice. A little girl stood with her mother in the audience around the house. Loudly, and in innocence, she said, "Is it them two lasses she wants? Them new lasses? They're up yon side of the rise, mam!"

Aunt's voice stopped. Kazy grabbed Beth's hand. "Run, Beth!"

They fled down the hill, over the ditch, and across the pasture. Kazy, her skirts held up in her free hand, ran on through the pain in her side and the rawness in her throat, not looking over her shoulder, gasping for breath. Beyond the pasture was a wood, and they ran on until they were sheltered deep in its leafy secrecy. Beth, released at last, flopped panting on the ground, and Kazy looked about her as her breathing calmed down and she tried to work out which way was which. They could not go back to Willowsford as long as there was any danger, but she could see an uphill path, which, if they took it, would give them a good view of the surrounding country and an idea of where they were. They were scratched, muddy, and breathless by the time they reached the top, but they were rewarded with sunshine and a clear view. They could see the patchwork fields and the Sheppard house, a long way away.

Beth, yawning, nestled against a fallen tree trunk and curled up like a cat, and Kazy settled beside her with the sun warm on her face as she closed her eyes. Which way to go? She imagined Aunt Latimer crashing about in the wood, laying about the undergrowth with a poker, appearing from behind trees and under bushes, whispering her name.

"Kazy!"

She had been falling asleep! She scrambled to her feet and turned to face the voice.

"Will!" For the sake of a friendly face she could have thrown her arms around him—but, of course, she didn't. "Will! How did you find us?"

"I reckoned you'd make for the wood, then the high ground." He flopped down and dumped a sack beside her. "God have mercy, Kazy, you might have told us she's as raving as a wolf. We called at your house and asked to speak to your father."

"How is he?" she asked eagerly.

"He's not there. He's gone to York to seek for you."

"Oh!" Kazy hadn't thought of that.

"When we first called, there was nobody at home," Will went on, "but we went back after market, and your aunt was there. She demanded to be brought to Willowsford, and as she was shouting and grabbing for the poker and threatening to fetch the magistrate, we did as she said. She muttered to herself all the way from Cutherham, and banged the cart with the whip handle and the poker every time we stopped. After that little lass in the crowd gave you away, she came storming out looking for you. She didn't get far. She slipped coming around by the cow shed and fell on her back. She wasn't hurt, but she got muddy from where you'd just scrubbed out the dairy. By the time she was up and in one piece, you were away. Eddie's taking her back to Cutherham now, but she's cursing and promising to come back for you. And she will, make no mistake."

Kazy stood looking at her hands, which were dirtier than ever in her life before. She rubbed at her fingers with great concentration.

"We've caused you a lot of trouble. I'm sorry."

Will looked at his feet. "It's all right," he said. "Only . . . only Mam and Dad have been talking about you. Mam says you can stay as long as you like, but Dad isn't pleased. He's had enough of your aunt. And . . ." He looked away. His voice became gruff and very low. "Your aunt says you steal."

Kazy felt the heat in her face.

"Will, look at me," she said. "I took my mother's jewelry and my musical instruments, and those are my own. And a little money that was mine, and Eliza's keys that are mine by right, though my aunt took them away. And food and drink that we would have had anyway."

"And a birch rod?"

"I burned it."

"You did what?" He gazed in admiration. "Well, here it is. Father's had enough of you and your aunt. He's scared that you could be taken up for witchcraft, and he doesn't want to be accused of harboring a witch." He scuffed the ground with the toe of his boot, looking at the boot and not at her, and finally said, "He'd have Beth, seeing as she's Eliza's child."

"Just Beth? Not me?"

Will nodded miserably.

"Beth?" Kazy knelt down in front of her and took her hands. "Beth, would you go back to Willowsford with Will?"

"Yes," said Beth simply and at once. "Are we going now?"

This was it, then. She had found a home for Beth. As for herself, something would turn up. She could find work somewhere or go home and face Aunt Latimer. Beth was safe, that was the main thing.

"Your cloaks are in there," said Will, pushing the sack toward her. "You'd best take yours out and leave hers. And there's some food in there. You'll need to take something to eat."

"Be a good girl now, Beth." Beth stood, pretty, grubby, and obedient, and Kazy made a pointless attempt to tidy her hair, if only as a way of keeping her for a moment longer. "A good girl, for your uncle and aunt. Kiss for Kazy?"

Beth gave her a dutiful kiss and a puzzled look, and Kazy tried not to think about losing her. Beth didn't appear at all upset. Perhaps, after all, they could live without each other, however impossible that seemed.

"Fare you well, Beth." Kazy smiled bravely. "And you, too, Will."

Beth gave a little shiver as if she'd just woken from a spell. "Aren't you c-co-coming, Kazy?"

"No, Beth, I can't. Go with Will."

"But you'll come later?"

"No, Beth, I've been too much trouble at Willowsford. But you can—Beth!"

Beth was shaking, and a long, high wail rose into the air, louder and louder. Her eyes filled and overflowed, and she howled.

"Bethy . . ." Kazy tried to take her hands, but Beth grabbed her by the waist and clung on as if she were drowning. Kazy looked at Will over the top of Beth's head.

"That settles that," said Will.

"Hush, Beth," said Kazy, rocking her. "I won't leave you. I don't know where we'll go. It'll be sleeping in haystacks again, and I don't know where we can buy food. If you stay here you'll have everything . . . There, now, you don't have to if you don't want to. Don't worry, Will, I'll find work some-where, somehow."

Will walked with them a little farther.

"The people who brought you in the cart, that's Ma and the tall tinker. His name's Diccon, but everyone calls him the tall tinker. They'll take you with them if you're prepared to earn your keep. The best thing to do, though, is ask them to take you to Collywell Cross. Remember that name. Collywell Cross. Master and Mistress Fairlamb live there."

"But where is it?"

"That's the trouble," admitted Will. "I don't really know. It's near either Abbey St. Andrew or Highbridge, I can't remember which. About ten miles north—or is it west?—of one or the other. Oh, but the tinkers are sure to know about it. I've never been there myself, but Aunt Eliza used to work there before she went to Cutherham. Every year she used to come and visit us, and she used to go to visit Collywell Cross, too."

Kazy could remember Eliza going away for a little while in the summer. She had never taken much interest in where she went or why.

"The thing is," said Will, "Aunt Eliza used to say that everyone is at home at Collywell Cross. The Fairlambs make everyone welcome, and whatever you need, that's where you'll find it. That's what she used to say, anyway. Now, do you see the path away to your right? That's the way to Corster. Ma and the tinker should be there by now."

"Will, you've been so good to us . . ."

Will shrugged and looked embarrassed. "Nothing to it," he said. "God speed you. And try to get to Collywell Cross. If you keep looking, you'll find it."

The horse was saddled, and Canon Clare made his farewells to his sister-in-law, Katherine Lawrence, at her grand house in York on a drizzly morning. Katherine had sent men of her own household to look for Kazy—one to London and one to the north—but they had reported no sign of her. Now he was going home to the cathedral, which no longer seemed important. Waiting for him would be only Joan and Matthew, glum and reproachful, and Frances, who was more terrifying every time he saw her. With a thin hope that Kazy and Beth might have returned, he rode for Cutherham.

The tinker, who preferred to be called Diccon, maneuvered the rattly cart along a rough track between one village and the next. "Call this a road?" he muttered. At last, he looked over his shoulder at Kazy.

"Can you drive a cart?"

"I can if you show me how," she said. So she sat up on the hard plank of the driver's seat while the tinker strode ahead, holding the bridle. Kazy wasn't sure what to think about him. Ma was big, comfortable, and easy. Diccon said little, smiled little, and took more interest in the horse and the goods than in Ma and the passengers. Still, if he was never merry, he was never angry, either, and Ma talked enough for both of them.

The horse had no intention of hurrying, and probably couldn't, even if it tried. So they rattled slowly through the lanes where the trees hung shadily over them, and the white umbel flowers brushing against the cart smelled sweet. Bales of cloth and boxes of trinkets rocked and jiggled gently, and so did Ma, who was making a pet of Beth.

"Can you remember now, Marian?"

"C-Co-Coddleham, Low Rock, High Rock," recited Beth. "P-Po-Postey . . ."

"Posley."

"Hilds . . . Hildsworth, Ladyhouse . . ."

" . . . then all the way to Highbridge!" they chanted together.

"And that place, Ka . . . Kate?" asked Beth. "C-Co-Cottycrosses?"

"Collywell Cross," called Kazy over her shoulder.

"Never heard of it," said Ma. "But you'll get work in Highbridge, don't you fret."

The cart lurched and tipped sideways, hurling Ma against the side. Beth, falling on top of her, had a soft landing, and Ma was well padded, but a wheel had slipped into a ditch, and they were stuck fast.

"Sorry!" called Kazy.

"You're allowed one mistake," grunted Diccon. "Only one. Call this a track?" He calmed the horse and took a kick at the cart. "All out."

Ma was clearly used to the cart falling in ditches. She scrambled out with a rattle of necklaces, and they heaved at the cart until it was free.

"Try again, Kate," he said. He put the reins back into her hands and let her drive all the way to Coddleham.

Coddleham was not much more than a cluster of houses and a street full of wandering poultry, but it was bigger than Willowsford, and there was a crowd around them before Kazy had even jumped down from the cart. Ma took a basket of ribbons, lace, and threads, and thrust it into her hands.

"Get them sold," she instructed, and added loudly, "Mind, it's all best quality." Kazy tried hard to remember all Ma had taught her about prices as the women jostled about her, picking up laces, quibbling over prices, and elbowing each other to get to the front. If she hadn't had her back to the cart she would have been knocked over, and an inquisitive chicken pecking at her foot didn't help.

"That's the price," said Kazy, when a sharp-faced woman tried to haggle with her. Canon Clare's daughter was not used to being argued with by a country woman. She looked to Ma for help, but Ma was too busy to notice, and the tinker had loaded up the horse with bolts of cloth to take to wealthier households.

"And what's the news, then?" asked an old woman, grinning through her jagged teeth.

"News?" faltered Kazy.

"News from Cutherham? Willowsford? What's the talk? Not much of a tinker, if you've no gossip!" She cackled as she sifted through the basket. "Nothing much worth buying in there, pet."

Ma appeared at Kazy's side, lifting the basket from her. "Play your pipe," she whispered. "At the market cross."

So Kazy stood on the steps of the cross and played every tune she could think of. It was a good move, because as long as she played the crowd hovered, unwilling to go home. The children and young women danced, and the more they stayed, the more they bought, until at last Ma took Beth by the hand and said, "Load up again. Diccon will be back shortly, and we'll get up to the farm."

They spent the rest of that day and the night at "the farm." It belonged to a wealthy yeoman who always offered Ma and Diccon a meal and a place to sleep. In return for this they helped in the fields, carried letters to Highbridge, and sold him cloth cheaply. It was nearly dark when Kazy came in, tired and aching, from haymaking, but Beth had been allowed to stay in the stable sorting out some trinkets that Diccon had carelessly dropped. They should have slept in the barn that night, but something in the straw bit Beth, so they curled up in the cart instead.

"I'm tired enough to sleep on a stone," said Kazy, and thought of her bed at Cutherham.

Rain set in the next day, and Low Rock and High Rock were such tiny villages that they sold very little. By the time they left High Rock Kazy no longer had any idea where they were, and, before long, she had something much more important to worry about.

Canon Clare strode into the parlor. He did not look at his sister, who sat straight as a post at the table. Joan hovered in the doorway.

"There is no more news," he said, speaking to Joan, and not to Mistress Latimer. "No further sightings of the girls since they left Willowsford."

Joan laid a hand on his arm. "Kazy got them both safe to Willowsford, sir, and she'll keep them safe. No harm will come to little Beth, sir, when her sister's got her."

"I don't know why you fuss," muttered Aunt Latimer. "They'll come home when the winter starts to bite. Kezia is an arrogant little piece, just like her mother. And the other one is as common as a servant." But she was muttering at the log basket, and nobody heard her.

It was two days' journey to Posley, a big village with a crossroads and an inn. Trade was good, Kazy played and sang and sold trimmings for all she was worth, and Diccon declared at last that they had earned enough to stay at the inn. Ma was majestic as she haggled with the landlord, insisting on a room well swept, with clean mattresses—she even inspected them for bugs—before taking the room. She added that the young ladies were used to sleeping clean and warm, and that supper must be brought to their room for them, because the rough company downstairs was not suitable for the young ladies.

They ate a hot meal in the upper room, and afterward Ma

and the tinker joined the company downstairs. Kazy and Beth were left alone to settle for the night.

"It would be nice to go home," said Beth, "if we could have home without Aunt Latimer."

A whole sentence without stammering! Kazy cuddled her.

"I know, Beth, I know. Don't settle down yet, we haven't said prayers." She wasn't at all sure what God would think about her running away, but she'd better try to keep in good favor with him.

Ma might have objected to the rowdy company for the girls, but she and the tinker were happy to join it. The raucous singing and laughter wafted upward, and it was a long time before Beth could sleep. Kazy herself was still awake when the door creaked open, and, by the light of a single candle, she could make out the figures of Ma and the tinker. In the dim light, she could see their faces. They were grim faces. Ma's voice was low and threatening.

"We want a word with you," she said.

It seemed a long time since they had first met Ma on a sunny day on the road to Willowsford, when she had seemed enormous and comforting. Now, she filled the doorway with threat, like Aunt Latimer. Kazy placed herself between Ma and Beth.

"Now, Ma, we'll sort this out," said Diccon, then spoke softly to Kazy. "Ma's upset. And she's had a drop more than she should. We need to talk, Kate."

"Kezz-*eye*-a," said Ma very deliberately. "Her name's Kezia."

"Maybe it is," said the tinker. "You see, at a place like this, with a crossroads, there's a chance to share a bit of talk and hear what's happening. And the gossip from Cutherham, young Kate, is that two young ladies are missing from the house of one of the clergy—not one of your penny-pinched parsons, mind, but a canon. Two girls, last heard of at Willowsford. One thirteen years, the other six. Dressed like gentlewomen. Speak like gentlewomen. Educated. You don't get many lasses like that."

There was no point in pretending anymore.

"You knew we were running away," said Kazy. "You guessed."

"We did. But most runaways are running from folks who don't care for them. Someone's looking for you."

Hope and fear sent a shiver through Kazy.

"My father? Is he looking for us?"

"Don't know 'bout your father, but somebody is," said Ma, and slouched against the wall. "There's a man been about on the roads asking for you. He says he comes from your aunt."

The thought that rage, not love, was seeking them out fell on Kazy like darkness. "It's my aunt we're running away from," she said.

"That's your problem," said the tinker. "Our problem is that we don't want to be taken up before the magistrate and put in prison for spiriting away a canon's daughters."

"But that wouldn't happen, would it?" It had never occurred to her.

"It's just what would happen, if they find you with us."

\

"But I'd speak for you, I'd tell the magistrate it wasn't your fault!"

"You know nothing of the world, young gentlewoman. If a tinker meets a magistrate, the tinker comes off worse."

"We'll leave, then," said Kazy. There seemed nothing else to do. "As soon as it's light, we'll make our own way to Highbridge."

"It'll look even worse for us," said the tinker, "if anyone's noticed that we've got two lasses with us, and suddenly you're off and away. That's almost proof of guilt, that is. No, we'll go on to Hildsworth and sell a bit, and while we're there you keep out of the way. Then straight to Highbridge, and, when we're there, lose yourselves."

"You're really kind, Diccon," said Kazy. "Thank you."

"You're real soft," sniffed Ma. "Hildsworth! I'll give you Hildsworth." But presently she was asleep and snoring like a well-fed sow.

But it wasn't Ma's snoring that kept Kazy awake. Aunt was looking for them. What about her father? Didn't he care?

Diccon thought it best that the girls should keep away from them in Hildsworth and meet them beyond it—"On this road, about half a mile yon side of the village, by the stricken tree. About the time them in the fields have had their bread and beer and gone back." Ma had warned them sternly not to go near the cart—"I don't want anyone thinking you're with us," she had said. So, as Ma and the tinker started selling, Kazy and Beth wandered along the edges of fields. Beyond the village was thick woodland as far as Kazy could see.

"W-w-why do you keep looking round?" asked Beth.

"I'm just looking," said Kazy shortly. They were out in the open and very vulnerable if someone really was seeking them. Towns and crowds felt safer.

"I'm thirsty," said Beth. "Is there anything to drink?"

"We'll have something later, on the way to Highbridge."

"But we-we-we'll go home one day, won't we?"

"One day, when I know Aunt Latimer won't beat you."

"W-w-when?"

"Look, Beth, have you seen the little cat on the wall?"

"Yes. When, Kazy?" Now that Beth was growing more confident and stammering less, she had resumed her old habit of continuous questions. Kazy had forgotten about that.

"Just when it is, Beth."

"I'm still thirsty. Oh!" Suddenly Beth's face grew pink, her hands flew to her mouth, and tears rose in her eyes. "I've left Maid Marian in the cart!" she wailed. "She might get sold!"

"Oh, Beth." Kazy pulled out a handkerchief, which was far grubbier than it had been in the Cutherham days. "Dry your eyes. I'll get her for you. I suppose if only one of us goes to the cart, it won't be noticed."

In the village, Ma, with a basket on her arm, was selling to passersby. Diccon had left the cart at the gates of a large house, almost opposite the churchyard, with a cover spread over the bales of cloth in case it rained.

"Play in the churchyard, Beth," said Kazy, "but keep out of sight."

Climbing into the cart, she found Maid Marian safely there. She put the doll in her own basket and filled their bottle with ale from the jar. The old horse pricked his ears and turned his head as she jumped down, and, as she stopped to pat his neck and brush the flies from his nose, she heard a voice.

"There's some better stuff in the cart—come and I'll show you!" It was Ma.

Kazy turned hot and cold. Ma was lumbering down the street, with a customer beside her! For a wild moment she hoped for a miracle, for Ma to vanish or collapse or disappear through a hole in the road, but Ma was too solid for any of that. She was glancing from side to side as she walked. The worst thing for Kazy to do would be to stay put.

She could hide in the cart, under some cloth—but no, Ma was going to show the customer some cloth. Under the cart? Too easily seen. There was the wall of the big house garden, and beside it an enormous beech tree, if only she could reach it without being noticed.

In the middle of the road a ginger cat lay stretched on its side and washing its ears. It rolled over and rubbed itself in the dust. Kazy ducked, picked up a pebble and spun it past the cat's nose, and, as the cat sprang after it and Ma and her customer turned their heads to look, she dashed for the wall. She tumbled over it, concealed herself deep in the branches, and hoped that Ma and her customer would be quick about their business.

The man at Ma's side was dressed plainly, but in good clothes, with a black cloak and very tall, gleaming boots. He was dark, with a strong beard, and looked respectable. Not a man to buy trinkets. Kazy listened, and as she listened she knew he did not want to buy anything from the cart at all.

"It seems most likely," he was saying. "Well-spoken girls? Dressed like gentlewomen?"

"With lace collars and cuffs and good cloaks. See, Master Challoner," insisted Ma, and she rummaged in the cart to find any of Kazy's belongings, "that's hers. Them's her recorders. That bottle's the one she had when we found them, and that's the bairn's doll. Do you recognize them?"

Kazy bit her knuckle and hated.

"I regret that I cannot recognize them," said the man. "I have not met the children. I am only an agent of their aunt."

A thin line of sweat ran down Kazy's neck. Go away, I hate you.

"We have settled to meet them," went on Ma, "at the stricken tree beyond the village, after midday. Now, Diccon, the tinker, has a kind heart to the girls, I don't know how he'll feel about parting with them . . ."

"I think the reward may persuade him," said the man rather grimly, as if he didn't really enjoy this. Maybe he's not cruel, thought Kazy, just a pleasant man with an unpleasant job. He looked trustworthy—but then, so did Ma.

"That's in advance," said the man, putting money into Ma's hand. "The rest when the children are in my hands."

He strode away, but Ma stayed to fiddle and fuss with the goods on the cart, almost as if she knew she was tormenting Kazy, who stood, white and tight-lipped, with her back pressed to the tree trunk. Even when Ma finally plodded away, she stopped in the street to look over her shoulder. When at last she was out of sight, Kazy sprang into the cart, gathered all that was hers and Beth's into her basket, crammed bread into the corners, and, though she was desperate to run, sauntered over the road so as not to attract attention. In the churchyard, Beth ran to cling to her. Her eyes were red and frightened in a blotchy face.

"I w-w-was scared! I thought Aunt Latimer had come to get you!"

"This way, Beth." Kazy bustled her through the churchyard to a track, which led through a field of cows, and eventually to the fringe of the forest. When they were concealed by the trees, she stopped.

"Drink this. Out of the bottle, but not too much, we have to make it last. We can't go back to the cart, Beth. I heard Ma talking to a man who came from Aunt Latimer. He's looking for us, and Ma wants to hand us over to him."

"But she's our friend!"

"Not now. We'll try this way. We'll find somewhere to go. Oh, I wish I knew how to find Collywell Cross."

She took Beth's hand and led her in the direction she thought must be south, but the need to find their way around bogs and thornbushes soon left her disoriented.

"It's all right, Beth," she said. "This is a friendly forest. It's keeping us safe. Do you see that little wren?"

"Don't worry, Beth," she said presently. There was some sort of a path, so they must be going somewhere. "Aren't we having a lovely walk? Look! There's a shrew! Are you tired, Beth?" she asked as Beth began to lean against her. "We'll rest soon. Do you think there are little animals watching us?"

"My feet are wet," sighed Beth.

"Look!" said Kazy. They had come to a sharp turn in the track, and the forest grew thinner ahead of them. There was a thin spiral of smoke, which might have come from a chimney. "Look, Beth! This way. This path must lead—Ow! You! Get off me! Let me go!"

There was no time to fight. Beth's hand was wrenched from hers, and strong arms held Kazy so tightly that her kicks and struggles were useless. In a sharp glance over her shoulder she met the face of a grinning youth, dirty and pimply with stubble on his face. Before her stood Ma, with Beth kicking and screaming in her arms.

"The lad here said you'd turn up here, sooner or later," said Ma. She took Beth, who was trying to bite her, and tucked her under one arm. "Now you're coming back to the village like good little lasses, back to your aunt's man, and you'll come quietly."

"We won't!" screamed Beth.

"You will or you'll get such a beating you'll limp for a month."

Kazy kicked. "Don't you touch her. Nobody beats Beth." Ma seemed to find this very amusing.

Think, Kazy told herself. You can't fight, you can't run, you can't threaten, and you daren't try the witch thing. Try reason.

"Why are you sending us back? Can't you see what our aunt will do to us?"

"That's your trouble, not mine. Tinker and I have lived hard a long time, and who's to keep us in our old age? There's a reward out for you, and I can't afford to miss out on a good trade. A fair price for the goods is all I want. Some of us live tough lives, young Canon Clare's daughter. Some of us make hard choices. Tinker's too soft to hand you over. I'm not."

"So it's just for the money."

Ma laughed as merrily as ever, as if they were all happily together in the cart.

"Of course it's the money! I have to make a living."

Sometimes, when Kazy had lain awake in the cart imagining the future, she had pictured herself selling her mother's jewelry to buy warm clothes for Beth in the winter or medicine to save her life. The thought of those softly glowing pearls in Ma's coarse hand was unbearable, so she tried not to think about it.

"If it's money you want, I can make a better trade," she said, and she looked up at the boy holding her. "Let me go, and shut your eyes."

"Do as she says," ordered Ma, and stared as Kazy hunted through her petticoats. "Well, if you'd said you was a treasure house!" She gawped at the pearl necklace like a child at sweetmeats, releasing Beth without another thought as she reached out her hand, and Kazy, clasping Beth tightly in her arms, watched Ma's face. She was weighing everything up—where to sell it, how much it would fetch, how best to use the money. It was clearly worth more than she had been offered by Aunt's messenger. It had looked so beautiful in her mother's portrait, but in Ma's rough fingers it seemed cheap and tawdry, like a toy.

At last, Ma nodded. "There's a village down there. Dead sort of place, poor and dirty and we don't bother with it, but I dare say you'll find somewhere to sleep. I'll have to get back to your aunt's man and tell him you gave me the slip."

"Ma," said Kazy as Ma turned to go, "if, after this, you betray us—if you think you can get the reward money as well and hand us over—I'll swear before a magistrate that you stole my necklace. And," she added to the lad, "that you helped. I'll swear it to anyone, on any oath, and I don't care if you hang for it. Do you understand?"

Ma gave a grudging nod, turning to go and wrapping the necklace carefully in her old pink kerchief—but Kazy was already leading Beth away and gulping down freedom like fresh air.

She learned something else new that day. She learned that distances, like people, could be hard to judge, and the chimney smoke, which looked so close was really miles away, and there was much struggling up and down and taking the long way around the bogs. A thin drizzle was falling.

"I wi-wi-wish we were home," said Beth, "but w-without Aunt Latimer."

It was a relief to hear Beth talk about home. Sometimes Kazy thought she had imagined a time when they lived at Cutherham, in a town house with a garden, and Joan to look after them, and a table with pewter plate, and their own bed-chamber. Now it seemed perfectly normal not to know where they would spend the night or where the next meal would come from. Perhaps she was more Kate than Kazy.

Damp, muddy, and tired, they came at last to a few tumble-down houses where the people looked at them with such resentment and distrust that Kazy didn't want to approach them. They were near coal mining country, and a layer of black dust seemed to have settled everywhere. On rising ground beyond them was a barn, but, when they approached it, it looked even worse than it did at a distance. There was a damp, unwholesome smell. A mangy cat with ragged ears and bald patches stalked toward the hay and emerged again with a rat kicking in its mouth. At least, though, they had a good view of the surrounding countryside. "There's a church," said Kazy.

"It's miles away!" wailed Beth.

"It's that or the barn."

"Heigh-ho!" sighed Beth, and Kazy laughed and hurt at the same time, because that was what Eliza used to say.

It was a squat little church with an oak-studded door, which was locked, but there was a tiny stone porch where they could shelter. It would have to do, as Beth could walk no farther, so Kazy spread her cloak on the floor of the dark, cobwebby porch. The Ten Commandments, in badly spaced lettering, were painted on the opposite wall. Whichever way she turned,

Kazy could feel those commandments watching her. A fire would have been nice—Diccon had taught her to light a fire—but she had no flint and no kindling. There was bread and cold meat, though, in the basket, and they settled down to a meal.

"Is this from the cart?" asked Beth.

"Yes, and don't talk while you're eating."

"Is it stealing?"

"No. We would have eaten it anyway. And we've worked for it. It wasn't my fault that we had to run away again."

There was a pause, and the silence felt as if it were waiting for something. Then Beth finally said what she wanted to say, but she whispered it so softly, with her fingers in front of her mouth, that Kazy had to ask her to repeat it.

"Is it my fault?" she whispered.

"Is what your fault?"

"Mother. Aunt Latimer. Running away . . ." There was a squeak and a snuffle, and Beth pulled the skirt of her gown up to her face. Kazy put her arms around her and held her very, very tightly.

"Nothing is your fault, Beth. Whoever is to blame for all this, it isn't you." It might be Aunt Latimer's fault, Father's, or her own, and sometimes she even felt angry with Eliza for dying. Beth was the only innocent one of them all.

"Sometimes," said Beth with a sniffle, "sometimes I've been naughty."

"We're all naughty sometimes. I promise you, it isn't your fault. Nobody thinks it is. Oh, Beth, if only I could find somewhere safe to stay. It's as if it isn't real. I suppose we'll just have to go to Highbridge, and I can find work there."

Beth nestled against her. "It's a shame about your jewels."

"I don't want them!" It made Kazy laugh. She would have fought for food or warmth or a safe place to live, but a string of pearls? "I don't need them. I still have the earrings and my mother's gold ring. And the keys to the house. And you."

"You looked lovely at home when you used to put your jewels on. Ma w-w-won't. She'll look fat and stupid."

"She won't wear them, she'll sell them."

"I hope she gets a bad bargain," sniffed Beth. "I hope she rolls off the cart and lands on her fat—"

"Beth! Eat your bread and be quiet. It'll be an uncomfortable night."

"Better than at home," said Beth, who seemed halfway between tears and ridiculous laughter, "on the floor on the prickly mats when I . . . you know . . . she wouldn't let me sleep in the bed."

"But I used to let you into the bed when she'd gone . . ."

". . . and sometimes she caught us . . ." Beth giggled.

". . . and then we both had to sleep on the floor . . ." Kazy was laughing, too.

". . . and then . . ."

". . . we got back into bed . . ."

". . . and if we got caught, we had a beating!" Even that sounded funny, now that it was a long way away.

"No more Aunt Latimer!" sang Beth.

"No more Aunt Latimer!" Kazy pulled the cloaks around

them. It may be cold and the floor was hard, but Beth had laughed, really laughed, and had said all that with hardly a stammer. Soon it would be dark, and she wouldn't be able to see those commandments.

Somewhere there really was a place called Collywell Cross, a place where Eliza had once lived, a place where they would be welcome. Will had talked about it, so it must be real, and sooner or later they must find it. She felt for her secret pocket. There were the keys to the house in Cutherham, keys she had used to get out in the hope of one day getting in again. There were the intricate pearl earrings. And there, at the heart of it, was the wedding ring, simple and beautiful. Father used to say a ring was a symbol of God, because it was a perfect whole, with no beginning and no end—but she didn't want to think about God just now.

"Strange thing," said Ma to the tinker. "Well, we waited and they never came."

"They took their things with them," said the tinker. "Mebbe they were on the run from that man. He was in the village today."

"Is that so?"

The tinker glanced at her, but she was looking into the distance.

"He asked me about them," said the tinker. "They might have given him the slip."

"Just as well," said Ma. "He would only have dragged them back to that old aunt in Cutherham."

"No," said the tinker. "He's not from the aunt in Cutherham. We shared some good ale and got talking. He's from their aunt in York. Mistress Lawrence of York. A wealthy woman and most concerned about them, it seems."

"Well!" said Ma, and went on looking into the distance.

"We're in a big white bed with curtains," said Kazy to Beth, who was cuddled tightly in her arms under the cloak. "We've got a fire in the grate, and the bed curtains are a little open so we can see the firelight, and the snow falling past the window, and . . ." but Beth was nearly asleep, with Maid Marian in her arms. Kazy could no longer see the commandments, but she could feel them. Thou shalt not steal, honor thy father and thy mother, thou shalt not bear false witness . . .

I haven't really stolen, she thought. And I've told lies, but not harmful ones. I don't think I'd really lie to a magistrate about Ma. And as to honoring my father and mother . . . I'm honoring my stepmother. I have to look after Beth for her. "I'm sorry, God," she whispered. "You'll have to look after yourself. Beth only has me."

In her chamber at Cutherham, Mistress Latimer sat up in bed, hugging her knees and frowning at the bed curtains. She was not on speaking terms with her brother. She had followed his miscreant daughters all the way to Willowsford and harangued the country idiots who had sheltered them. Was Walter grateful? Her headaches were bad. Did he not remember she had headaches?

In the future, let him run after his own daughters. The house was quieter without them.

"Kazy! Wake up!" urged Beth.

Kazy woke from a light sleep in which she still felt cold. She sat up shivering and aching with stiffness.

"There's a man in the churchyard!"

Kazy scrambled up, pulling Beth back from the doorway. "What sort of a man?"

"Just a man. I think he . . ." Beth's voice trailed into silence. A tall figure blocked the light from the doorway.

6

A scarecrow, thought Kazy. A scarecrow parson, tall and stooping and so thin she felt sorry for him. His gray hair was wispy, but clean, and his large, bony hands trembled a little. The clerical gown he wore, like everything about him, was threadbare, and his lined face had the look of a baby bird, gawky and hopeful and almost comical, except for his eyes. There was something about his eyes—kindness, yes, and wisdom, but something else, deeper and harder to name—something that reminded Kazy of her father.

"Have you been here all night?" He was well-spoken and anxious.

"We're just going," said Kazy, still shivering. "We're on the way to . . ." she couldn't think of anything else, "Highbridge."

"My dear, you are far out of your way. And you're only children."

"I'm fifteen," she lied easily. "I look after my sister." She curtsied to show that, with respect, it was time to go. "Good day, sir."

"But I can't let you go out hungry after a cold night! My name is Thomas Pettigrew, I have the care of this parish. The parsonage is not far."

Beth looked hopefully at Kazy, and Kazy looked at Thomas Pettigrew. It was part of his duty as a clergyman to offer hospitality, and he was very like her father. Her father had let her down, though, and so had most of the people she trusted. But the appeal in Beth's eyes won, and they went with him. Kazy, afraid that Beth would say too much, took over the conversation.

"Do you live alone at the parsonage, sir?"

"I have a wife," he said, and there was an awkward pause. "She is not in good health. But look—there is the parsonage!"

"Isn't it little!" exclaimed Beth. Kazy glared at her, but it was the truth. Inside, it was plain and sparse as the priest himself—clean, with little furniture, and a single room serving as kitchen and parlor. A door led from it to what she supposed must be the bedchamber. There was a scrap of a fire in the hearth, and already Beth was warming herself. Master Pettigrew himself gave them bowls of hot porridge—there was no sign of a servant—and seemed content that they should eat and drink without fuss. But when Kazy took out her recorder to make sure it was dry and undamaged, his deep eyes brightened.

"Do you play? Will you play now, please?"

So she played, and Master Pettigrew pottered happily about the kitchen. At some point he must have opened the small door, for Kazy noticed it standing open, just a little. Soon Beth, filled with warm porridge, was yawning by the fire like a sleepy kitten, and Kazy, too, realized what a rough, cold night they had spent. She closed her eyes and was nearly asleep when a moaning sound disturbed her. At first she thought Beth was having a nightmare, but as she opened her eyes she knew it was not Beth. In the adjoining room, somebody had cried out in distress. It was too late to blame herself, and say that they should never have come here. Picking up the poker, she tiptoed to the door and looked in.

In the plain, bare room stood a bed with its faded old curtains drawn back. Propped up on the pillows was a woman so pale and haggard that she looked as if death had already marked her and was waiting to complete what had been started. Her hand, lying on the coverlet, was tight, like a claw, and gray hair trailed on the pillows. On the bed beside her sat Master Pettigrew, patiently feeding her with porridge from a spoon. A surge of pain must have risen in her and she gave a soft moan, then a louder one, turning her head this way and that on the pillows, fighting the cries, and Master Pettigrew put down the bowl and folded her in his arms.

"My love, my love," he was murmuring, and his face contracted as if he felt her pain, too. "If I could bear this for you, I would. It will pass. It will pass." As the pain subsided, he laid her back on the pillows and stroked back her hair before he took up the bowl again.

Kazy drew back from the door, but she still listened.

"As soon as you are comfortable," he was saying, "I will ride south. This will be so good for us, Grace. If they are Canon Clare's daughters—and I am sure they are—we will be rewarded for this. No, my dear, they are not poor little mites at all! I have met Walter Clare, he is a good, kind man. They have nothing to fear in returning to him."

A tired voice said slowly, "Then why did they leave?"

"Oh, some misunderstanding, no doubt. I will speak to him on their behalf. Where else could they go? I found them sleeping on the porch!"

There was a muffled cry of pain, which hurt Kazy to hear. When Eliza was dying—no, she would not think of Eliza, crying out and dying in a room they were forbidden to enter so that they would not catch the fever. But this woman did not have a fever. Some creeping disease was eating away her life.

"There will be money to pay the physician, Grace. For all the medicines and sleeping draughts you need and firewood and sea coal. You need never again lie in a damp room with no fire. You will be well."

Kazy tiptoed to the fireside where Beth lay sleeping. Everything ran against them, everything was complicated, except Beth. Beth had been as bright and true as mother's gold ring, until Aunt Latimer came. She would be again, one day, because at heart she was still Beth. Kazy sat down beside her and put her head on her knees.

She could tell Master Pettigrew everything and beg him not to give them away—but it would be cruel to ask him to choose between their safety and the money he needed so much. She could stay, to be caught and taken home to Aunt Latimer.

The floorboards creaked. She curled onto the floor and pretended to be asleep, because it was easier to do that than to look Master Pettigrew in the face. Presently she heard a shutting of doors. He had gone to alert her father, or maybe to find Master Challoner, her aunt's messenger. Warm, lovely Beth lay curled beside her, and a gray woman gasped in pain in the next room. And Kazy remembered their bedchamber at Cutherham, on the morning of their escape, as she looked out at the towers of Cutherham Cathedral and made her solemn vow.

She played one more tune, hoping Grace Pettigrew would like it.

The silence in his cold little house did not altogether surprise Thomas Pettigrew. It had been too good to be true, too much to hope that the reward for the Clare sisters would fall into his hands and solve all his problems.

On the table lay a linen napkin from the children's basket with a message on it. One of his own quills lay beside it. He read, "You have been kind to us. If you knew all, you would not want us to go back, but I hope you will convey our love to our father. I have left something under this napkin, to thank you for your care. Please sell these to buy whatever you need for Mistress Pettigrew."

On the table lay a pair of pearl earrings—small, elegant, and strangely lovely in the dim kitchen. Thomas Pettigrew raised the back of his hand to his eyes, but the only sound was a stifled groan from the next room.

In the doorway, the tall man in the black cloak stood still. He would not intrude on a man's grief and a woman's pain.

"Don't drag your feet, Beth."

Beth stopped hanging back, did a little trot to run ahead, and kicked a tuft of grass.

"I wanted to stay." She sniffed, and, as Kazy took no notice, did it again, more loudly. "I can't walk another step."

She sat down on a stone by the roadside, folded her arms, and pouted. Kazy wanted to laugh.

"Good-bye, then, Beth," she said, and kept walking. When Eliza used to do that it had seemed rather harsh, but it worked. It worked this time, too. Beth was soon trotting up behind her, and a cart was drawing near—but Kazy only asked the carter for directions to Highbridge—"And how long is it to walk there, please?" and they walked on.

As soon as the cart was out of sight, Kazy looked about her and took Beth's hand.

"If this is the Highbridge Road, and that's the River Tarl," she said, "Abbey St. Andrew must be the other way. Come out of sight of the road, Beth, we'll follow the river as far as we can."

"Aren't we going to Highbridge?"

"No, because everyone who's met us thinks we are. If anyone asks that carter, he'll say we were on our way to Highbridge. So will Master Pettigrew. So we're going to Abbey St. Andrew instead."

Though she said nothing to Beth, she was wishing they had

run away to the Lawrences in York instead of the Sheppards in Willowsford. It was too late, though, for that. They walked all day. Kazy cut a hole in Beth's shoe, where it dug into her foot. Their way led across the moors, which felt eerie and deserted, with only a few sheep to notice them. At evening, they found a very small hut—it was, in fact, a hut used by shepherds at lambing time—to spend the night in. The last shepherd to use it had left flints and kindling, and they found enough wood to make a fire. After a few unsuccessful attempts, there was a crackle of twigs and leaves that brightened their faces, and when Beth was asleep, Kazy said a prayer for Thomas Pettigrew, and for his wife, and watched as the glow faded from the pile of ashes. She imagined a place where there would be clean, warm beds, hot meals, and kindness. But everyone she met seemed determined to send them back to Aunt Latimer. Why should it ever be different?

Beth's voice woke her in the morning. She sounded sharp and cross.

"Go away! This minute!"

Kazy sprang up, hitting her head hard on the low roof so that her eyes watered. In the doorway, Beth was dismissing a large and inquisitive sheep.

"It's gone," she said proudly. "I frightened it."

Kazy rubbed her head. "You frightened me," she said crossly. "I thought we were being attacked."

Beth pouted. "So? You don't always have to be the brave one."

Beth was becoming more like her old self every day. And

that, thought Kazy, is what she needs, so I'll just have to get used to Beth's old self. There was a breakfast of very dry bread and water, and a long walk. Hardly any food was left. Kazy had no idea how far it was to Abbey St. Andrew, and by midday, Beth was begging for a rest. They were high on the moors, and there was very little shelter from the sun.

"Let's get to the top of this hill," said Kazy. "I'll be the horse and you be the cart." It was another of Eliza's methods. She reached her hands behind her as Eliza used to do, and pulled Beth along, though the sweat prickled and her legs ached, and when they reached the hilltop . . .

"Oh! Beth, look! That must be Abbey St. Andrew!"

Below them, sheltered by the hills and bounded by the River Tarl, the town of Abbey St. Andrew lay contentedly in the valley. The gray old abbey with its square tower was surrounded by rows of little houses, as if it had gathered its children around its feet. In front of it was a wide, empty forecourt and a paved rectangle, which, from their viewpoint, looked like the board for a game, though Kazy knew it must be the marketplace. More closely packed streets arranged themselves around it, and wiggly lanes trailed off toward the river.

"Are we going *there?*" asked Beth in delight.

"Yes, Beth. It looks like home, doesn't it?" Kazy was remembering, powerfully and painfully, that she was a town girl, and this was her first sight of a town since they left Cutherham, so long ago. It might have been months, or years.

It was farther than it looked, and there was much slithering on loose stone and grass on the downhill journey. At a clear, fast stream they stopped to wash their hands and faces, and

Kazy, remembering what Ma had said about lace collars and cuffs, removed them from their gowns. It made them look a bit more like servants. There must be somewhere, thought Kazy, somewhere we can spend the night in Abbey St. Andrew, and somewhere I can work, if we ever get there, if this moor doesn't go on forever, and a dozen kinds of curses on these stones, and never mind, Beth, we'll get you new shoes in Abbey St. Andrew. By the time Beth had been carried, then walked, then carried again, they could see more people than sheep, and there was town chatter all around them, and they passed under the great stone gate into Abbey St. Andrew.

"What's that smell?" asked Beth loudly.

"All towns smell like that," said Kazy, who had forgotten how towns smelled, especially in summer—human and animal dirt, staleness, baking bread and meat, sweat and spices. "Now, Beth. Who am I? That's right, Kate. And how old am I?"

"Fifteen. I'm Marian. Can I be seven?"

"I suppose so."

"Eight?" she tried her best smile.

"You don't look eight. Our parents are dead, and we come from—oh, Willowsford, I suppose."

In the busy marketplace they looked about at the houses and shops, cramped higgledy-piggledy like bad teeth, on three sides. On the fourth side stood the abbey, nothing as grand as Cutherham Cathedral, but ancient and stately. Perhaps someone could tell them how to get to Collywell Cross—but the thought of another long walk was too much, even for Kazy. A row of cobblers' and glovers' workshops stood opposite, but she turned her back on it.

"Cobblers' shops and glovers smell horrible," she said, "because of the skins and the glue. Let's try the jeweler."

But the woman at the jeweler's shop was not eager to employ a lassie of whom she knew nothing, with a useless child trailing behind her. Nor was the tailor, nor the hatter, nor even, when she felt forced to try there, the cobblers and glovers.

"Send the bairn to its granny, and I'll take you," said a dirty old shoemaker with an evil grin, and he chuckled as Kazy grabbed Beth's hand and ran out of the house.

"I should try somewhere better than this," said Kazy, when they were outside. "There must be a big house with lots of servants, if we can find it."

"Is there anything to eat?" asked Beth timidly, as if she knew there wouldn't be. "I'm hungry."

Kazy was hungry, too. She had a little money, but she would need to make it last. She bought bread, and they sat down on the steps of the tall stone cross in the marketplace to eat and rest their feet.

"We will find somewhere, won't we?" asked Beth.

"Of course we will," said Kazy, because they had to. "There's always the inn. Inns aren't pleasant places to live, but they must need servants."

"Kazy!"

The sound of her own name came to her as if in a dream, and she thought she had imagined it. But it came again, a real, happy boy's voice, and a fair-haired young figure was running toward them.

"Will!" cried Kazy. "Beth, it's Will Sheppard!"

At the sight of their cousin's smiling face in this strange town, Kazy forgot her tired feet and hunger. Sitting at the market cross, she told him all that had happened, and how they needed work.

"You'll not find it easy," he said. He looked grown up in his working clothes with his bag of tools over his shoulder. "Most people take servants they already know about, local people, except at the hiring fair. The next hiring fair's at Martinmas, and that's months away. Let's think." He frowned. "My master and the mistress don't need a maid. There's the curate from the abbey . . ."

"The last clergyman who helped us was about to hand us over. Has anyone been asking about us?"

Will shrugged. "Someone came asking questions when I first arrived, but nothing since. So, as they've searched here and gone away, they're not likely to come back. You're as safe here as anywhere for the moment, if you can get a roof over your heads."

He frowned thoughtfully, and as he did so a girl, dark and strikingly good-looking, came out from the apothecary's shop. She carried her head high and swung her hips, and the basket rocked on her arm. Will jumped to his feet.

"That's it! Mad Jennet!" He waved at the girl. "Martha! Martha, come here!"

The girl who sauntered toward him looked down at Beth and Kazy as if they were something left over on a market stall, but as Will explained that Kazy wanted work she smiled with welcome.

"You want a place? You can have mine! I've got another to go to, soon as there's someone to look after Jennet. It's a good place."

So good that you can't wait to leave it, thought Kazy. But she needed the work.

"My little sister would have to come, too," she said. Martha shrugged.

"Jennet won't care. It's a cushy place. There's just Jennet to look after, and it's a small house, and she's not over fussy. You even get your butter and cheese and stuff brought in from the farm."

Will grinned. "Tell her about Jennet."

"Jennet's no harm," she said, a little too quickly. "She's daft, but she's harmless."

Beth pointed and giggled. "Who's that?"

Kazy followed her gaze and saw a small, elderly woman, dressed as if for a pageant in a blue gown with tattered lace at the sleeves. Her hair looked neatly curled until, as she came closer, it proved to be a badly fitting wig, with a faded blue lace-trimmed cap perched on top of it. Her shoes were blue, too, with silver buckles, and far too elegant for the marketplace. She approached Martha with a tottering walk, as if her knees were bound together.

"Annie?" she said. Her voice was high and demanding, but not very confident. "You are Annie, are you not?"

Martha laughed. "Oh, I'm Annie today, am I? Yes, I'm Annie, then. Shall we go home, Jennet?" She took the old woman's arm and looked over her shoulder at Kazy. "Annie today. Yesterday, I was Sarah. You may as well come."

"We'll follow you presently," said Will. When Martha and Jennet were out of the way, he sat down by Kazy. "I'll have to get back soon to Master Norris—that's my master. I'll tell you this quickly. Jennet's as mad as the north wind. She goes wandering off, any time of the day or night, and she has to be watched—she's no danger to anyone else, but she might come to harm if she wanders away. She forgets what day it is, what time it is, and who you are. Every girl who ever worked for her left before long in case they turned as wild-witted as she is. But she never strikes a servant or anything of that sort. Sooner or later she'll have to go and live with her daughter, then you'll be free to go and find Collywell Cross—or you could do what Martha's doing now, and pass her on to somebody else if you can't stand her any longer. Could you live with a madwoman?"

"I'm running away from a madwoman," said Kazy. "This one sounds all right."

Behind the abbey lay a winding row of old-fashioned houses with their upper stories jutting across the lane. Will led them to the end house and banged on the door.

"I'll leave you to Martha," he said. "And if you need me, I'm apprenticed with Master Norris, end of the lane, turn right. Only . . ."

"Don't worry," said Kazy, "we'll pretend we never met you before today."

Pushing open the door, she found Martha on her hands and knees, rubbing the floor with a cloth. There was a strong, unpleasantly sweet smell about the house that reminded Kazy of something, but she didn't know what.

"I can be out of here on Monday," said Martha, glancing up. "I've got another place to go to."

"We need somewhere to stay straightaway," said Kazy.

Martha sat back on her heels and shrugged. "You and the bairn? I don't suppose Jennet will mind. There's just her chamber and a small room upstairs, but you two can sleep in here until I've moved out."

When Kazy finally did settle down that night, on cloaks spread in front of the kitchen hearth, she felt she had been in Jennet's house for weeks. She knew where everything was kept and how to make porridge for the morning. She knew when market day was and that sometimes Jennet would give her money for the marketing, and sometimes she would forget. "But you'll get it sooner or later," said Martha, "when she remembers where she's put it." She had learned where to fetch water—"The abbey well is best, especially in summer." She knew to keep the food covered away from the mice. She had learned, too, the source of the strange smell.

"She wets the floor," said Martha, "and the bed. You just have to keep some water heating. I hope you don't mind washing."

All this instruction had taken place with constant interruptions. Jennet would decide to go out, and Martha would insist that she stay and eat her supper, and a dozen times Jennet would look up suddenly and ask, "Who are you? Oh. Is Martha leaving us, then? What did you say your name was?"

"She can't help it," said Martha. "She forgets as soon as you tell her."

At last, Martha put a drop of strong liquor in Jennet's warm milk to make her sleep, settled her down for the night, and said, "I'll tell you a bit about Jennet."

Jennet had been married to a wealthy glover and was now a widow. Of her family, only a daughter survived, and she was married to a rich yeoman farmer whose land was some miles beyond the town. This daughter and her husband had urged Jennet to live with them, but she was so determined to stay in her own house that whenever the move was suggested she locked the doors and hid under the table. Once, her daughter had come to collect her, but Jennet's hysterical screaming had brought the whole town running in the hope of watching a fight. Since then, the daughter—Mistress Philipson—had contented herself with sending provisions from the farm every week.

"All good, and plenty of it," said Martha. "It's a good place, Philipson's. That's where I'm going to work. They said

I can go there as soon as I will, if there's someone here for Jennet. The plowman comes every market day, that's on a Monday. He'll take me up there."

Kazy tried to remember everything Martha had said—market on a Monday, don't buy the fowls in summer, they stink and have things crawling in them. Remember, you always need hot water in this house. There's a woman at the market who sells soap . . . Kazy supposed she'd manage somehow.

Canon Hunt looked at Canon Clare, and Canon Clare looked out of the window, as if he were afraid of missing something.

"I said," repeated Canon Hunt, "that we are to have a new bishop before the year is out. The king has made an appointment."

"I heard you," said Walter Clare, without interest.

"Walter, listen. Our new bishop is something of a Puritan, and I swear the dean will find him impossible to work with. We will need a new dean." He placed himself between Canon Clare and the window. "Walter, it has been said for years that you should be the next dean of Cutherham."

"I hardly think," said Walter, "that I should take charge of Cutherham Cathedral. I can't even control my own family. No, Nicholas."

"Cutherham needs you. Only you can keep the canons all speaking civilly to each other. You are the most dedicated of us all."

"No," said Walter sadly. "I have hidden in my work. I hid from my grief and from my daughters, and even, yes, from my sister. That is not dedication. Do I deserve to be the dean?

Do you think I care who is dean of Cutherham? Now, to more important matters, Nicholas. Do you know of a parish priest in this diocese, named Pettigrew?"

Kazy learned quickly. Martha would grin as she watched her slowly peeling onions or scraping burned stew from the pot.

"You haven't done much of this kind of work, have you? Never mind, you'll soon learn. And Mistress Norris will keep you right. She pokes her nose in, but she's kind."

Kazy did not want to be "kept right" by Mistress Norris, the short, neat, bustling wife of Will's employer. She mistrusted this woman, who had already called twice "to see if all's well" and asked Beth and Kazy a lot of questions about themselves. Beth lied so perfectly that Kazy felt proud of her and ashamed at the same time.

On market day Martha was to leave, and the grumble of cart wheels woke Kazy early. The protesting bleats, squawks, and lowing of the livestock came next, so she could hardly hear Jennet speak as she helped her to dress.

"I think the blue gown would be pleasant for a change, Sarah," said Jennet, and Kazy didn't bother to tell her that she'd got the wrong name again, and that she'd worn the blue gown every day this week. "And my best lace cap." Jennet liked her finery. "Who is that child?"

"That's Marian."

"Oh. Marian. Yes. She's ours, isn't she?"

Kazy didn't like that idea. It was as if Jennet was taking over Beth. But it was important that she accepted her.

"Yes. She's ours."

Martha guided Kazy around the market that day, while Beth tagged along and Jennet tottered after them, chattering loudly all the time. By the time the carts were loading and getting ready to go, Martha's belongings were in a bundle and Martha was almost dancing in her eagerness to leave. A secretive grin passed between Martha and the wagoner as he helped her up, and Kazy knew exactly why she was so keen to go.

Back in the house, Kazy surveyed the parlor. She was the queen of her realm now, with this house to run and Beth and Jennet to care for. Beth would sleep in the small room, and she herself would take the trundle bed in Jennet's chamber.

In the cool larder stood the basket of provisions from the farm, with a smooth creamy cheese in the center and a glowing nest of plums. It had been a tiring day, and there was still the larder to tidy. Should she just serve bread, cheese, and cold meat for supper, and some of these plums? She turned to ask Martha, but, of course, there was no Martha to ask.

When Beth had been asleep for hours, and Jennet had been put to bed for the second time and seemed likely to stay there, Kazy searched through wooden chests and cupboards until she found paper, a little ink, and a not too scratchy pen. Then she lit a rushlight and, after much thought and trying out different sentences, began to write.

> Father,
> I have a home now, for Beth and myself. I know I have grieved you and been a bad daughter, but how else could I look after her?

If you will have us home, and if you will not let Aunt Latimer ill-treat us, ask for us in Abbey St. Andrew. We will never submit to her again.

I will trust NO MESSENGER, but only yourself.

I pray you are well.

Kezia

She read her letter again. It was probably foolish to risk everything by sending this letter, but she had to try. If her father forgave her, he would fetch them home, and not let Aunt Latimer rule over them. If they were delivered into Aunt's hands again, they knew how to run away.

Twice in the night Jennet woke her, thinking it was morning, and Kazy would have slept late if not for Beth waking her up. As soon as Jennet had dressed and breakfasted, Kazy hurried out in the hope that any remaining market men might be leaving the tavern, but it was too late to find anyone to carry her letter to Cutherham. She returned to find a neighbor's cat in the larder, smugly licking butter from its whiskers, and Jennet asking when it would be breakfast time. She had forgotten breakfast already.

The following weeks were harder work than Kazy had ever known. She made a reasonable attempt at keeping house, and Beth helped. The food she cooked was never as good as Joan's and always came late to the table, but it was edible. She became used to the nasty jobs, like emptying chamber pots, and the heavy ones, like carrying water, and she was learning to wash clothes. What made life almost impossible was the way every task was broken up with a dozen interruptions. She would have to leave the bread half kneaded because Jennet had wet her clothes again. She would look up to see Jennet wandering alone into the town, and by the time she had brought her home the fire would be out and the water in the pot no longer boiling. She would fetch water from the abbey well and come home to find Jennet thinking it was nighttime, and getting ready for bed. And there were the same questions, hour after hour: "What is your name? Are you my new servant? Have we had supper yet? What day is it today? Are you Sarah?"

At Cutherham, Joan had always looked neat. Kazy wondered how. It was all she could ever do to brush the flour from her gown, the dirt from her face, and the coal dust from her hands, which grew sore with washing. Her own hair became straggly, and Beth's was wild. At night she was almost too tired to go to bed, and in the morning she was more asleep than awake when she helped Jennet to dress. There was rarely time for Beth's lessons, and Kazy worried about her. Jennet adored her like a granddaughter, and Beth was usually sorting Jennet's threads or playing to her on the recorder when Kazy wanted her to help in the kitchen.

Beth came readily to carry water from the abbey well, though. Now that she was no longer so shy, she looked forward to the chance to play with the other children at the market cross. They often met Will there, too, and it was Will who found someone to carry Kazy's letter to Cutherham. They could never talk for long, though, because Jennet always appeared at these times, wearing the strangest assortment of clothes and looking for Sarah or Martha or even Kate.

Aunt Latimer stood by the window and squinted upward. Nobody wrote a clear, neat hand anymore, and all letters must be held to the light. The boy who delivered this one had actually told her that he was only to give it to Canon Clare, and she had told him sharply that she was capable of handing a letter to her own brother. The impudence of the young! And here was another one, young Kezia, dictating her terms for a return home! She could just picture that spoiled, overeducated child with her insolent way of looking you in the face.

It was not as if Kezia was even wanted at home! Life was much simpler and quieter without her opinions and her shrill pipes and clattering virginals, and that other one, always laughing or crying or running about, the silly brat of Walter's servant.

There was no need to trouble Walter with this letter. He would soon become accustomed to living without those girls. Unaware that she was muttering to herself, she knelt stiffly and held the letter to the fire.

The early mornings were cool, and Kazy made porridge, which, thick and disgusting as it looked, was easily made and warmed their insides. It stuck to the pot, though, and she stood scouring with reddened hands when there was a knock at the door. She rubbed her hands on her stained apron, expecting Mistress Norris, who was always turning up "to see if you're managing." But it was Will, with a basket of dark plums.

"The mistress sent these," he said cheerfully. "She would have brought them herself, but she's having a cleaning fit. I'm to take the basket back."

He stayed to help Kazy transfer the plums to a bowl in the kitchen. Beth put her head around the door.

"Hello, Will!" she said. "Jennet's puddled again."

Kazy gave her a plum. "Eat that and be quiet. And find her a clean petticoat, please."

Jennet tottered into the kitchen and peered at them.

"Are you Sarah?"

"No, I'm Kate. You need a dry petticoat, don't you?"

"Do I? Oh. Where are my petticoats?"

"Marian will find you one."

"Oh, yes. Marian. My little girl."

She pottered away with Beth. Kazy took a cloth to mop the floor and a handful of dry strewing herbs to disguise the smell. "Jennet's making a pet of Beth. Please, Will, this time, don't go away until you've told me about Collywell Cross. I can't go on forever cleaning up after Jennet. I know somebody has to, but it doesn't have to be me."

Jennet appeared again.

"She's my granddaughter, isn't she?"

Kazy wrung the cloth very tightly. "Yes, Jennet, your granddaughter. Off you go with her. That's right. Now, Will, Collywell Cross."

"It's somewhere off the road to Westhaven, I think," said Will vaguely. "Of course, I've never been there. It was a monastery once, and it was supposed to have a healing well. After the monasteries were destroyed it was sold, and had lots of owners until it was bought by Hugh Fairlamb and his wife. He'd already made wagonloads of money out of shipping coal. Like I told you, Aunt Eliza worked there when she was younger. The thing is, the Fairlambs—that's Master Hugh and Mistress Mary—she said they were the kindest people she ever met. She really loved Mistress Fairlamb, she used to go all that way to visit her every year. They take in more servants than they really need, and teach them weaving, careful management of the household and farm, how to make medicines, all sorts of things. They help find apprenticeships—that was how I got mine. They've restored the monastery chapel, and they all get together for prayers there. They'd look after you both. They'd sort things out with your father. They're kind people."

They are too good to be true, thought Kazy. They have to be.

"We don't need looking after," she said. "I look after us. And as for kind people, the last kind person I met tried to hand us over. My father's kind and he couldn't see what was going on in his own house. Being kind isn't enough, Will. When I meet kind people, I take Beth's hand and run."

Beth appeared in the doorway, holding a shoe and walking lopsided.

"Kazy, I mean Kate, can you mend my shoe again?"

"Again? Let me see it. Good-bye, Will. Thank Mistress Norris for the plums."

The next market day was blustery and cool, and the market men and women cursed as the gusty breeze wasted the flour and made the animals restless. Jennet had passed such a jittery night that at last Kazy had given up trying to go back to sleep. She had risen, dressed Jennet, and set the water to heat.

"Is it market day?" asked Beth, when she came down.

"Yes. Help me tidy the pantry, ready for whatever the farm sends."

Beth helped happily in the pantry, sweeping the shelves clean so they would be ready for the new provisions. She coughed so that her eyes watered.

"It's the flour," she gasped, coughing and laughing at the same time.

Kazy wasn't sure. Lately, she had forgotten about Beth's coughs. Now she remembered how she had coughed so long and so roughly that it seemed her throat would tear apart, and Eliza, anxious and trying to hide it, holding a cup to her mouth. "Take a little sip, now, Beth, just one. Little sips, little breaths, now." She remembered, too, the smell of thyme and honey. Thyme grew in the neglected garden, but honey was more of a problem. Beth's coughing calmed down at last, but Kazy wouldn't let her near the flour dust again.

"I'll buy honey at the market," she said, "if Jennet knows where she's put the money."

"Can I get some new shoes?" asked Beth hopefully. "My old ones are almost in pieces."

Kazy wanted to say yes—Jennet would certainly allow money for shoes for Beth—but the sound of gusting wind outside changed her mind. "I can't take you out in this, Beth. It's windy out there, and all the dust and dirt are blowing about. You'd cough more than ever. I'll bring you back some honey."

Kazy's own shoes were worn, too, and she had taken to wearing an old pair of Jennet's, too big, but adequate, when she went to the market. The cheapest honey was mostly wax, and it took some searching and haggling before she struggled home with dust blowing in her eyes and straggles of hair whipping across her face.

"Marian! Jennet!" she called as she opened the door. But her voice sounded strange and lonely. She left the basket on the table and ran to the yard, the parlor, the bedchambers—

Jennet and Beth were gone.

$\mathcal{A}$ new bishop would soon arrive in Cutherham. Walter Clare tried to be interested. Nicholas Hunt always accompanied him home these days, knowing how much he hated to enter the house alone.

"They are not in Highbridge," Canon Clare was saying. "But there is news. Challoner has searched for them in Highbridge. Two different jewelers say they were offered a pearl necklace for sale . . ." his voice became low and grave, ". . . by a tinker's woman. This may be the woman Kazy and Beth were seen with." He walked to the fireplace and stared toward the grate.

"There must be many tinkers and many necklaces," said Canon Hunt.

"A big woman. And a very fine necklace. They refused to take it, believing it to be stolen." There was fear in his eyes, and he turned away and looked at the ashes in the grate. "If these are Kazy's pearls, the pearls that belonged to her own mother, she would not part with them easily. Kazy has not written to me, though she promised she would. What would an unscrupulous woman do for a valuable necklace? Kazy and my little Beth are silent, Nicholas! They—"

He broke off. Then he was on his knees in the grate, scrabbling in the warm ashes.

"Walter, what are you—"

"Here! Here! See this, Nicholas!"

Nicholas Hunt peered at a charred scrap of paper in his friend's grimy fingers. He could make out "ther" and "nger" and nothing else, but Walter Clare's hand was shaking.

"Kazy's handwriting!" he was crying. "This is Kazy's writing!" He scrabbled in the grate again, not noticing the heat of the bars and the ashes. "And here, too! This is Beth's name!" He flung open the kitchen door. "Frances! Joan! Matthew!"

Joan came in from the yard, frowning and ready to be scolded. "Matthew," she said coldly, "is at the blacksmith's, and Mistress Latimer has gone to the apothecary again."

"Joan, did you light a fire in here this morning?"

"I did not," said Joan, who would not take the blame for whatever Mistress Latimer had been up to. "Mistress Latimer insisted on doing it herself. I said if she must have a fire I'd make one, but she said she would just do it. And let it go straight out again, I see."

"Did you see her burn anything? Has anyone called?"

"Not today, sir. Matthew saw someone at the door yesterday, shortly before supper, but it was nobody he knew."

"Thank you, Joan." He waited until she had left the room.

"A letter, Nicholas, from Kazy. Perhaps you should go. I would not have you here when my sister returns home."

In Abbey St. Andrew a driving rain was lashing the almost deserted market and tattering Kazy's hair as she ran through the streets. She had searched the marketplace, she had called at the Norris household, she had asked strangers in the street. Yes, Jennet and Beth had been seen. The cobbler had sold Jennet a very nice pair of shoes for the little lass. They had bought gingerbread in the market. They had taken the west road out of the town, toward Prior's Hill—but Kazy had climbed to the top of the hill and not found them, and now her skirts were heavy and sodden with rain, her cheeks were stinging, she was wet to her skin, and still no Beth. No Jennet. Perhaps I shall never see my Beth again. She even ran into the abbey, in the faint hope that they might have sheltered there, but there was no Jennet, no Beth. She stood in the doorway, her wet clothes clinging coldly, her teeth chattering.

"Dear God," she said in her head, "I know I've broken your rules, but I've done it for Beth, and now I want you to do something for her, please. Please, please, bring her home safely. It isn't much to ask. Just bring her home. And," she added, "Jennet."

One more call at the Norris house might help. She ran across the marketplace, but a farmer loading his cart stopped her.

"You still looking for the old woman and the little lass? They went that way. Not long since."

Home! She gathered up her gown and ran without stopping to Jennet's house, the wet skirts slapping her ankles and rain dashing in her face until she crossed her own threshold and Beth, straggle-haired but safe, was running to meet her.

Kazy held her very tightly and very long, pressing her cheek against Beth's wet head as if she wanted Beth to melt into her and never go away again, and Beth clung, too, though Kazy was wringing wet. As they let go of each other, Beth smiled bravely, turned her head away to cough, then said, "New shoes, Kazy! Look!"

"Beth, where have you been? I've been out searching all day. I've been so—"

"Marian?" came Jennet's shrill voice. "Marian? Shall we go and buy shoes?"

She stood fidgeting in the doorway, her gown damp at the hem and ridiculous pink ribbons lopsided in her cap. "It's time to go."

"Be quiet!" snapped Kazy, so sharply that Jennet shuffled back into the doorway, and Beth looked up in alarm. "Beth, tell me where you've been."

So Beth told her, with a lot of hair twisting and coughing, how Jennet had announced, just after Kazy went to the market, that they were going out to buy shoes. ". . . and I told her to wait for you, but you know what she's like, and we went out, and I got new shoes, look!" Jennet had bought her fruit and gingerbread and insisted that they visit the abbey, but they had to leave, Beth said, because Jennet wouldn't keep quiet. Then Jennet had decided on a walk to Prior's Hill. ". . . and I had to go with her, Kazy, to look after her." They had been stranded on Prior's Hill when the rain started but Beth, remembering her earlier experiences, had found a shepherd's hut to shelter in. "And we stayed there waiting for the rain to stop, but it wouldn't, and Jennet kept wandering off, and I thought I'd never get home, and I was frightened—but not much . . ." she finished, with a coughing fit so violent that her eyes watered.

Kazy's hands tightened.

"Beth," she said quietly, "don't you ever go off with Jennet again. Promise?"

She did not wait to hear Beth promise. She went to the parlor where Jennet, who was fussing with a basket of threads, looked up vaguely.

"Are you Martha? Or are you Kate? Make the supper."

Relief gave way to anger in Kazy. She closed the door, which would never quite shut properly, and found her hands were shaking.

"Jennet, don't you ever, ever take my sister out again. You don't care what happens to her, do you? She's coughing, she gets bad coughs in the winters, and you think she's your pet, but she's my sister, and you could have lost her, and I don't care how old or frail or dithery you are, nobody, nobody, *nobody* treats my sister like that, do you understand, you vain, selfish old woman!"

Jennet looked at her as if this were some stray cat spitting at her. "Get out of my house!" she ordered crossly. But Kazy swung the door and strode back to the kitchen. She made sure that Beth's clothes were dry, then she pulled off her own wet gown, spread it before the fire, and she stood in her gently steaming petticoat. They heard the front door open and close.

"She's gone out," Beth reproached her. "She might get lost."

"I hope she falls down the well," snapped Kazy.

"You're horrid," said Beth suddenly. "She meant no harm. I took care of her, I found the little hut and kept us safe, don't you think that was good? You could say something! You were really cruel to Jennet just now. Sometimes you're just like Aunt Latimer!"

"Bethy!"

Beth heard the tearful note in Kazy's voice and ran to put her arms around her—but Kazy turned away and rearranged the wet dress before the fire, and there was a long, uneasy silence between them until they heard Jennet, escorted by Master Norris, shuffle back home. Only then did Kazy remember that none of them had eaten since breakfast, and she began wearily to set out a meal of bread, cheese, and cold meat because she was too tired and hungry to bother with cooking anything. They all ate in the kitchen, and nobody seemed to mind.

Kazy lay awake that night, listening to Beth's coughing and wondering what to do if she became seriously ill. She thought of Beth's outburst of temper that afternoon. Now that Beth was confident enough to talk and to laugh, she must be able to be angry, too, to argue and be difficult. She relived the afternoon, and the fear of not knowing where Beth was, and whether she was safe.

That's what I've done to my father, thought Kazy. She sat

up in bed, hugging her knees. If I could get to Collywell Cross—and if they're really as good as Will says—they'd understand and put things right. But I don't know how to get there, and I can't leave Jennet.

Joan spent the evening in the kitchen, dipping rush plants in tallow to make rushlights and folding linen and wishing that Canon Clare would shout. All evening she had heard his steady, quiet anger and Mistress Latimer's nervous replies.

"Frances, do yourself the honor of telling the truth. I have fragments of Kazy's letter from the grate. How did they come there?"

"How should I know? Ask Joan, or Matthew." Then, as he remained silent, and she knew she must say something, "I had to destroy the letter. They were cruel, wicked words. I burned them to spare your distress."

"If they were the most profane words ever written, they were written to me, Frances, not to you. Where are my daughters?"

"She did not say."

"I do not believe you."

Cold anger failed. So did pleading, and demanding, and attempting to catch her in a lie.

"I do not know where they are. I do not wish to."

In the morning Mistress Latimer, muttering to herself, left the house and presently a cart was sent for. Only when her possessions had been removed did Joan dare to speak to Canon Clare.

"Where will she go, sir?"

"She will impose herself on her late husband's family," he said grimly. "I wish I cared. But all I care about is . . ."

"Yes, sir. I know."

It was two days since Beth had fallen ill, nearly three—or was it? Kazy was losing count of days and nights. She could hear her coughing and crying, but she heard that all the time now, in her head, even when Beth was asleep.

The abbey clock struck five, and Kazy had not been to bed. Beth had lain all the previous day and all this night, coughing violently and wheezing and crying out. She shivered, but her skin was hot. She would eat nothing, but Kazy stirred a little honey into hot milk and persuaded her to sip at it.

Jennet had been put to bed three times. Twice she had tried to light the kitchen fire. The third time she was brought home by the night watch, having wandered out of the house and gone to tell them that troopers were riding out to raid the town. It was only then that Kazy realized she had left the front door unbolted and the remains of their last meal on the table. The milk had grown blue and sour.

In the warm room, with the blankets heaped about her, Beth was not crying anymore.

She lay tightly curled in the bed, shivering so badly her teeth chattered. Occasionally, she whimpered. Was it like this when Eliza was . . . She must not think of Eliza dying. All day Kazy scurried from one task to another, and even the simplest tasks—scrubbing down the table, feeding the kitchen fire— were interrupted while she bent over Beth, soothing her and bathing her hot face. She had no idea why her face should be bathed, but it was what Eliza used to do. Then there was Jennet, questioning and demanding. As the day cooled and the twilight grew, she stayed as long as she could beside Beth.

"Stay alive for me," she whispered, though Beth never seemed to hear her. "I don't want to go on without you. If you die, it will be my fault. If you die, I'll go to Aunt Latimer and she can beat me to death if she wants to."

"Have I had supper yet, Sarah?" asked Jennet. So Kazy reluctantly left Beth and put together some sort of a meal for Jennet, but when she went up again, Beth's breathing was worse. Every breath seemed a painful effort.

Kazy's hands shook. She took a spoonful of honey and forced it between Beth's dry lips.

I need Father, she thought. Eliza, Mother, help me! Beth's mother, my mother, any mother, can't you see us? Any mother! Even Mistress Norris! She'd know what to do, but I can't fetch her. I can't leave Beth. Dear God, you're so powerful, won't you do something?

She tried to gather Beth in her arms to carry her to Mistress Norris, but Beth shook and whimpered and gasped so desperately that Kazy was afraid to move her. She stayed beside her, holding her hand, praying and singing Eliza's little songs and wishing she could wake up and find it was yesterday. No, not yesterday, last week. No, back to before they ran away. No, further back than that, back to before the winter, when Eliza was alive. Sweat broke out on Beth's face. Kazy held her hand tightly. She slipped her free hand into her mouth and bit hard on her knuckles.

Please, Beth, she thought. Please, please, God.

There was a sound of tottering footsteps. Jennet hobbled into the room, and her voice was high and petulant.

"Sarah! Sarah! Why have you not cleared the parlor? What an idle girl! Where are my gloves? I want to go out. Oh!" She peered over the bed. "What child is that? What is the matter with her?"

It was more than Kazy could stand.

"Leave her alone, you stupid old woman! She's dying because you took her out in the rain and I'm sick of your fussing and your questions and just leave her alone and I hate you!"

She waited for Jennet to hit her or order her out of the house. But Jennet merely pottered away without a word and left Kazy ashamed. It was due to Jennet that they had a home at all, and she was fond of Beth. She sat and sang one of Eliza's lullabies, to soothe Beth and keep herself awake. She was still awake, but only just, when there was a firm step on the stair, and Mistress Norris appeared in the doorway.

"God have mercy, what's this? Here's Jennet saying the little one's dead and the maid's run mad! Here, let me see."

Mistress Norris was quick and keen-eyed at the bedside, feeling Beth's face and hands, looking for rashes and peering into her eyes and mouth. At last, she smoothed the covers and straightened herself up.

"She'll do," she said confidently. "She's having a good sweat. That's as it should be. A bit of goose grease on her chest and she'll be well enough, but mind, she'll be a wan little thing for many days yet. You should have called me before this."

"I couldn't leave her. And Jennet . . ." Kazy bit her lip hard.

"Now, lass," said Mistress Norris kindly, "all places have their own little sicknesses, and the bairns here all catch something like this. I daresay your sister gets coughs every winter, but she's strong and always been well cared for, I think. But what about you? When did you last have a proper night's sleep? Not since you've been with Jennet, I'm sure. Here, let me settle her for the night. I'll call in the morning."

Kazy was never sure what Mistress Norris put in Jennet's sleeping draught that night, but they all slept soundly. In the morning Beth, though still weak and coughing, was no longer feverish, and Mistress Norris applied a nasty-smelling ointment to her chest and back.

"I need to go to the abbey well," said Kazy. "Will you stay with her, please?"

The well lay behind the abbey in what had once been the garden, and, as she crossed the forecourt, she remembered the day when she had stood in the doorway, drenched and terrified, praying for Beth to be safe. Perhaps God had answered her prayer, in spite of all the bad things she'd done, and she should go in again to give thanks. She slipped through the dark porch, paused as her eyes grew accustomed to the dimness, and pushed open the heavy door to the dark, cold abbey.

It felt as if the angels had left it and blown out the candles. It was plain, gray, and solid, with none of the glory of Cutherham Cathedral. To the left rose a staircase, which used to connect the abbey with the monks' dormitories, and to the right, half screened by the door, a seat had been carved into the thickness of the wall. In the dark corner it was well hidden, and Kazy wriggled into it to say a prayer. She could hear voices as two men made their way down the stairs, and, as they came closer, she shrank back into the shadows. Then she gave a shiver of surprise, drew up her knees, and held herself completely still. She had recognized a voice.

"Can we not persuade you to stay longer?" said one voice, probably the rector.

"I have been too long already. We must prepare for the coming of the new bishop."

It was Canon Hunt, her father's friend! She shivered again and bit her knuckle.

"And you may have a new dean, I believe," continued the rector. He had a pompous voice, as if he were too pleased with himself. "Is anyone . . . ?"

"As to that," said Canon Hunt, "it was always said that Walter Clare would be the man."

"That Canon Clare whose daughters . . . ?"

"The same," said Canon Hunt gravely. "He thinks of nothing else. But he has been a wretchedly changed man since his wife died."

The rector's voice took on a high, rather teasing note. "He married a servant, did he not?"

"He married *my* servant," said Canon Hunt firmly. "An excellent girl, and a joy to him and to young Kezia. Kezia was born of his first marriage."

They paused to continue their conversation at the door. They were so close, Kazy thought they must hear her breathing.

"And his first wife was . . . ?"

"Kezia Patterson. Bishop Patterson's daughter."

"Good God in heaven! That Kezia Patterson? The one they called the Holy Amazon? They say she spat fire, and spat it in Greek! Is it true she spoke five languages and argued with her father in four of them?"

"Certainly, she was a spirited young lady. Her father took an interest in Walter Clare, became his patron, and secured him a place as a canon of Cutherham. Kezia took a greater interest in him, and, as usual, got what she wanted. She died giving birth to young Kezia, who is very like her."

"Another such! Poor Clare!"

"Canon Clare," said Nicholas Hunt firmly, "is in a hard way at present. There has been a quarrel with his sister, who at last packed up her belongings and left his house in a high temper."

Kazy lifted her head, and her heart lifted, too, as the weeks of struggling fell from her like a damp cloak slipping to the floor. Aunt had left, and they could go home!

The door creaked. The footsteps were moving away, but she could still hear the voice of Canon Hunt.

"But," he was saying, "he has brought her back now. Mistress Latimer is under his roof again and will stay there."

The door banged shut. Kazy hugged her knees, put her head down, and sat very tightly curled and silent. If the world was to end, it might as well end now.

"Mercy on us, Kate, where have you been?" Mistress Norris sprang to her feet as Kazy trudged into the small chamber. "I haven't all day to sit . . . and the look of you, girl! What's happened to you?"

"Nothing," said Kazy. "Nothing. How's Marian?" Sitting on the bed, she folded her arms gently around the only family she had left, and rocked her. "I do ask your pardon, Mistress Norris. I was delayed." She couldn't afford to lose friends now.

"Here she is!" In the early morning, Will stood grinning on the doorstep with Jennet. She was wearing an old-fashioned gown, a man's cap, and no shoes. He looked at Kazy, and his smile dropped. "What's the matter, Kazy?"

"I'm Kate," she said. "Or Martha or Sarah or anything. Not Kazy Clare anymore. Come in, Will. Have you had breakfast?"

He had, but she seemed not to hear him, and he ate the porridge she put down in front of him without arguing. Kazy sorted out a pair of stockings from a heap of dry washing and held them before the fire.

"You look as if you haven't slept all night," said Will.

"Jennet had me up twice. Once she tried to climb out of the window, then she came down here to light the fire. That's what she seems to like just now. But I couldn't sleep." And she told him, slowly and a little shakily, all that she had heard in the abbey.

"So that's that," she said at last. "Aunt Latimer left, and now she's back again. He never came looking for me. He didn't answer my letter, and I even told him where we were, but he's fetched Aunt Latimer back home. He knows that we can't all live in the same house, and he's chosen her. He's disowned us, Will. I never thought he'd do that."

"Perhaps there's been a quarrel, and she's agreed to treat you better if you do go home. Maybe she's changed, and your father's going to come looking for you."

"If he cared, he would have answered my letter. I've just hurt him too badly, and he can't forgive me, and I didn't mean that to happen. Sit down, Jennet, dear, get warm, and have your breakfast. It's as if Kazy Clare has sunk into a gray sea and drowned. I will be Kate forever. And the worst of it is, he doesn't want Beth, either, and she doesn't know, and I can't tell her." She pressed her hands hard against her face, screwed up her eyes tightly, then busied herself over sorting out the basket of firewood.

"For the fiftieth time, Kazy," said Will with exasperation, "go to Collywell Cross! I've told you, the Fairlambs will help."

"I know," she said. "But there's Jennet. She's driving me witless, but she needs me. Besides, I still don't know exactly where it is."

For the first time since she had known him, Will was angry. "Haven't you tried to find out? You've been here for weeks now. Do you mean you couldn't just gossip with people in the marketplace and say, 'Please, do you know of Collywell Cross, and how I could get there?' You could find someone else for Jennet. Mary Fairlamb could arrange something for her, if you asked her. You just don't want to go there, do you?"

She spoke very carefully. She didn't want a row with Will.

"I do want to. I want it because of Eliza. The more Beth comes alive, the more I can see Eliza in her. I carry Eliza's keys around with me, because it's as if I still have something to do with her, the same as I carry my mother's wedding ring. Collywell Cross is like Eliza's keys. I want it because it's something to do with Eliza."

"Well, go there, then!"

"But it'll be a disappointment, because I won't find her there. She's dead, and she'll stay dead, and Collywell Cross won't bring her back."

"Neither will staying here!"

"I know that, and I'd love to go somewhere I could get a good night's sleep, and Beth would be looked after properly. But the trouble with helpful people is that they do help, and they always think they know best."

"And of course, Kazy, they don't. You do." Will stood up and glared across at her. "Jennet's like a child. You're completely the mistress here, and you want to stay that way, so you won't let anyone help you, even though Beth gets ill and you can't cope. Well, I've got work to do."

"Will!" But he had walked out, banging the door.

It was time to help Jennet dress. There was no time to run after Will and say what she really meant. She said it in her head, as if he were there.

"It isn't easy, Will. If I go to Collywell Cross, they'll make me face up to everything I've done. The mistakes, the lies, everything. It's the place where I'll have to face the truth, and I don't know if I can."

9

"That lass has lost all the spring out of her step," observed Mistress Norris to a friend in the marketplace. It was an autumn day, and she was watching Kazy at a market stall. Beth stood behind her, holding Jennet's hand.

"She's made fine work of caring for Jennet," went on Mistress Norris, "and lasted longer than most maids do in that house." She dug her elbow into the ribs of a tall man in a dark cloak who was standing, she felt, too close to her. "I'm sure there's breeding there. They both speak very clear, and Kate had fine hands before the work roughened them. You know, in a house like Jennet's—with Jennet being the way she is—it's a house where the maid is the mistress." She liked this expression and repeated it. "A house where the maid is the mistress. Not all young lasses can manage that, but this one carries on as if she was born to it. But I do think . . ." she glared at the tall man, but, as his back was now turned to her, it had no effect,

". . . our young Will hangs around her far too much. He's just a lad, and she's fifteen. Or so she says!" She laughed loudly. When did a girl ever tell the truth about her age?

"What a foolish man," said Jennet to Kazy as they went home. "He asked me who Marian was, and of course I told him she was my granddaughter. Anyone can see she's my granddaughter. She's as like me as a twin, is she not, Martha?"

"Yes, of course," said Kazy gently, because she had learned to ignore Jennet's ramblings.

Kazy lay heavy with sleep, but something was tugging her into waking, something that should disturb her enough to get her up and out of bed. But she was so sleepy, for Jennet was worse than ever at nights. All was quiet, and presently she was dreaming.

There was bread in the baker's big oven, which seemed to have moved into Jennet's kitchen. She knew the bread must come out now or it would burn, but Jennet was taking her up to Prior's Hill, and they were lost . . . then she was back in the house again, and the bread smelled burned, but she had to find Beth, who had set off for Collywell Cross . . . then she was bringing Beth home, but Jennet's house was now the Cutherham house, and still the bread was burning and smoke was curling from the oven door.

She sat up reluctantly, half awake, rubbing her eyes, and reaching for the keys, for she always slept with Jennet's keys and Eliza's keys beside her. Of course she wasn't baking bread. But the smell of smoke was real.

"Jennet!" She stumbled in the dark to Jennet's bed, but it was empty, and the coverlet was gone. Feeling the walls, she found her way downstairs and saw the glow around the kitchen door. A crackling noise of fire reached her, and a stronger smell of smoke, which brought fear with it. She opened the door as little as she could.

Jennet had lit a fire, which filled the hearth space and spilled over onto the floor, where kindling wood lay on the rushes. Flames darted up the chimney, and the clothes Kazy had left airing by the fire were smoldering. In the center of this, Jennet stood with her coverlet wrapped about her like a royal robe. She smiled a calm, foolish smile.

"I have lit the fire for you," she said, as if Kazy should be pleased. The draft from the doorway was fanning the flames. Kazy prickled with sweat.

"Come here, Jennet, quickly."

Jennet still smiled and stretched out her hand. "Come and get warm, Kate." The coverlet slipped from her shoulders and flames from the kindling licked at it. Kazy ran and pulled her to the door.

"Out! The house is on fire!" With Jennet resisting and whimpering, Kazy put both arms around her and forced her from the room, but as she pushed the door the sudden draft swept up the flames. There was a roar and a crackle and a surge of heat, and with a shriek Kazy pushed the door shut— but that door never did shut properly, and there was still a crack. Fearing another draft, she opened the front door just enough to push Jennet through it.

"The watch, Jennet! Fetch the night watch! The house is on fire!"

Jennet, standing in the unlit street in her nightgown, did not move. Then, "I know what to do," she said calmly. "I'll fetch the night watch." She hobbled into the distance, and Kazy ran two at a time up the stairs.

"Beth! Wake up! Fire!" Beth was still half asleep with her thumb in her mouth and her arm around Maid Marian as Kazy dragged her from the bed. The sound of fire from downstairs was louder, and, not daring to risk the stairs, she carried Beth to Jennet's chamber window. Flinging it open, she screamed into the raw night air.

"Fire! Help! Fire! Beth, wake up and shout! Fire!" Her voice sounded thin against the night and the noise of fire. She banged on the wall joining their house to the next, and, tripping over Jennet's shoes, banged again with those. "Help! Help! Fire! Shout, Beth! Oh, dear God, if you ever loved us! Mother, Eliza, can you hear me? Help us! Fire!"

Beth rubbed her eyes and looked blearily out of the window. "There's a fire, Kazy," she yawned. "Is that what you want?"

Kazy followed her gaze into the night. Someone was bringing a torch—then there was another, there were footsteps, then the voice of the watchman . . .

". . . yes, Mistress Jennet, I know. Just you come home. Your Kate left the door unlocked again, has she? You come with me and—great God! It really is on fire!"

The fierce glow from the kitchen and the torches cast firelight on the street. Kazy could see a blanket held beneath them and the faces, orange in the blaze, looking up.

"Now, Beth," she said, "jump!"

"No!" screamed Beth, and clung to her with both hands.

"Jump or I push you. One, two, three . . ." but Beth could not be pried off, and to jump with Beth in her arms would be too dangerous. Trying again to unclasp the clutching fists, Kazy found the old wooden shape of Maid Marian in the crook of Beth's arm and wrenched it away.

"Beth, look—there goes Maid Marian!" She flung the doll from the window and, as Beth reached out, Kazy pushed. She watched until Beth was clear of the blanket before she climbed onto the sill and jumped.

The dawn was a gray, creeping thing, but Kazy welcomed it after the night. It was a dawn that looked drained of all its color, and that was how Kazy felt, too. Such a slow dawn that it was a long time before she could clearly see the shriveled hand that lay in hers. She felt again for a pulse.

In all that long night, since she first woke to the smell of smoke, Kazy had not slept. Exhaustion had made her eyelids droop time and again, but as soon as she drifted into sleep the nightmares swarmed in; fire, and falling, and then . . .

And then the part where she woke with a cry, as they both used to, in the days when Aunt Latimer had ruled over them. She didn't even need nightmares to bring back the scene. She had already lived it over and over again, wishing something could be different, only, she told herself, nothing that has happened can be different. It's like Father catching fever and Eliza dying of it, it's like running away from the only parent you have left. There's no changing the past, but that doesn't stop the wishing.

In no time she had tumbled from the blanket, and Beth was in her arms. But when she had looked up from Beth's curly head she had seen—oh, dear God, no!

"Jennet!" Already hoarse, she had screamed again. "Jennet! No!" There was Jennet, tottering up to the glowing frame of her own front door, as if she could not even see the flames, let alone feel them.

"Jennet!" Kazy ran, but Will had caught her and held her back, ignoring her kicks and struggles as bystanders ran to pull Jennet away.

"My little Marian is in there!" wailed Jennet, and through the shouts and the roar of fire came her shrill voice, "Get Marian out! Get her out!" She had escaped her rescuers, and Kazy was fighting wildly to reach her, when the door collapsed in a shower of sparks and burned wood scattered into the crowd.

Kazy stroked the thin hand. There had been plenty of willing helpers to beat out the smoldering nightgown and salve the burns, but Jennet was already frail without this. So now Kazy sat awake beside her as Jennet, calmed at last by one of Mistress Norris's sleeping draughts, slept soundly.

So, after all this, they had no home, no work, and, it seemed, no father to seek them and take them home. She had tried to care for Jennet. She had vowed to care for Beth. Now Jennet was injured and Beth, in the trundle bed upstairs, coughed in her sleep because the smoke had irritated her lungs.

The household was stirring now. Mistress Norris was on her way down.

"Now, Kate," she said sensibly as she bent over Jennet, "we must talk of your future. Jennet will just have to go to her daughter now. I've a sister in Highbridge who'll find work for you, and the rector will seek someone to look after your sister. Jennet's awful poorly, but she'll live, I think. You've done well with her." She opened the front door and frowned with disfavor on a bundle lying outside until she realized what it was.

"Kate, the watchman's brought your things here. It'll just be whatever they've got from the house, and don't you go trying to go back for anything else, for it'll all come down round your head if you try it."

"Everything came down round my head in January," said Kazy, "when my stepmother died." Just being able to talk about Eliza was something. But Mistress Norris was not listening, and Kazy began to sift through the bundle of belongings, some damp, some singed.

Her gown and Beth's were there, and their shoes. Their cloaks. Her recorders, wrapped in her gown, had survived, and Beth's petticoat. Eliza's keys lay before her, like a cruel joke.

She searched through the heap again, slowly, one item at a time. Then she remembered that her own petticoat, with its secret pocket, had been damp at the hem yesterday. She had left it in the kitchen to dry. There hadn't been much in the pocket. A few pennies. Her mother's wedding ring. Her father was lost to her, her vow on that ring was in ruins, and the wedding ring was melted, probably. Certainly, it was lost for ever.

"Thank you for being kind to us, Mistress Norris," she said, "but Beth and I have somewhere to go."

In the marketplace, Kazy found the man who regularly drove a cart from Abbey St. Andrew to Westhaven. She was lifting Beth over the wheel when Will came running across the marketplace to them.

"Will!" Then she remembered how she had hit out and struggled the night before. "Will, I'm really sorry . . ."

"Think nothing of it. I've had worse bruises."

"And the last time I talked to you, about Collywell Cross—and we argued . . ."

"Did we? Doesn't matter."

"And, Will, if anyone comes looking for us—I mean, if Master Norris finds out that you're my cousin—I mean, Beth's cousin—and you knew all the time who we were, it might look bad for you."

"Aye, well, I dare say I'll get away with a beating. It'll all be well, given time."

"You're a good friend, Will. And we're going to Collywell Cross. The carter doesn't know exactly where it is, but he thinks it's about five miles north from the fork in the road."

"Are you coming, or aren't you?" demanded the carter.

"Move, lass. Safe journey."

"God bless you, Will."

Then the cart rumbled away, and they looked back, waving, until Will was out of sight. Then Kazy turned her face to the rising moors beyond Abbey St. Andrew as she rode into a damp gray morning, to face the truth.

The grayness turned to a mist that veiled the road ahead and left a soft shining of droplets on Beth's hair, and on the spiderwebs in the hedges. Leaning against her, Beth, still weak from her illness and worn out from the night's alarms, was listless and silent. When they reached the fork in the road, the carter pulled on the reins and pointed out the way they should take.

"You want the northward track about five miles, it's off there somewhere. Or so I'm told. If you follow the Tangle, you'll not go far wrong."

"The Tangle?" asked Kazy.

"The stream, that's the Tangle. Do you lasses know nothing?"

Kazy looked up at a rising tide of moorland, wilder and sparser than any she had yet seen. It was a rough land of gorse and boulders, with grazing only for a few sheep who seemed not to mind thistles. And why, whenever she had to face a long, rough walk with a tired sister, did it always start to rain?

"Kazy, it's that way," said Beth.

"I know. I'll be the horse."

But the broken night soon caught up on Beth. By the time she had snagged her dress on a few thistles, been nettle-stung, tripped on stones, and dropped Maid Marian in the Tangle— Kazy had to climb down and fish her out—she had very little spirit left.

"Her paint's all wet!" wailed Beth. Kazy rubbed the doll on her cloak.

"We can do something about her when we get there."

"I'm too tired!"

"When we get around this little bend, we'll have a rest," coaxed Kazy. She was trying hard to be gentle with Beth, and it took her mind off her own weariness and hunger. Somehow, breakfast had been forgotten in the morning. She helped Beth over the bumps and boulders of the track, but when she looked up she gave a cry that was both delight and dismay. She could see Collywell Cross.

Delight, because, when she saw it, she wanted with all her heart to be there. Dismay, because it looked so far away.

She could see that the long, low building before her must be the back of the house. She could see a paved yard and a row of stable buildings, with the high windows and pale stone of the house and a tower beyond. The Tangle wound down below the house, and there were outbuildings to the north and south and an orchard. The orchard alone was enough to urge her on, but Beth was lolling against her with her eyes half closed, and Kazy hadn't the heart to force her. She settled against a tree with Beth in her arms, and, in spite of the damp grass, drifted into the dream in which Jennet's house was burning again. She woke suddenly, crying out, and stood up squirming as her damp clothes rearranged themselves about her. Beth coughed harshly in her sleep, and Kazy was filled with guilt.

"I should never have let you get so damp," she said. "Not far now. I'll carry you, if you can't go on."

With their bundle over her shoulder and Beth on her hip she set off, slithering on damp grass. With every step, Beth grew heavier, and her cough jolted her so badly that Kazy stumbled. It would take a long time. One more step. The next step. The next. Just as far as that tree. As far as that stone. Now rest, and count to a hundred. Now, Beth, walk a little. Just as far as that bush. Then I'll carry you again. Look back and see how far we've come. One more step, one more. Don't look to see how far it is, look at how far we've come. Up again, Beth. One more step. Just the next tree. I wish my hair didn't drip into my face. One more step. I have been walking forever.

Mary Fairlamb had made sure that all windows were closed and no roofs leaking. She looked out at the garden and smiled, because rain was needed. The lashing of the storm against the windows did not trouble her, because she knew it would soon rage itself out. She had seen over fifty years of storm and sunshine, and lived in a calmness deeper and firmer than the earth beneath her, but something was tugging at her heart. She walked without haste to the front of the house and looked along the track and saw it empty. All the same, she made sure that there was hot water, for she had a feeling that she would need it, and she silently offered a prayer for all travelers and homeless ones in the storm. Then she returned to her task of making healing salves. She was glad to hear the knocking at the door, when it finally came.

A dark, bedraggled girl, her face rain-streaked and her clothes dirty and dripping, stood gasping with cold on the doorstep. In her eyes was a spirit of struggle that struck to Mary's heart, and with all the strength left to her she carried a child held tightly in her arms. She was fierce and desperate, like a mother cat rescuing her kitten. Mary held out her arms.

Kazy's arms no longer ached, because she could not feel them. There was only rain and cold and the need to hold Beth. Then the door opened on a hall full of light, and a woman, clean and dry with a warm, kind face, opened the door for them. Kazy stumbled over the threshold and tried to speak, but she was too cold to manage the words. The sudden warmth and light startled her. And seeing a woman whose face was all kindness, and who was, above all, dry and safe, she surrendered Beth into the outstretched arms. For a moment it was enough, to stay wet and cold and speechless, and to see Beth wrapped in enfolding love.

That night, in a clean white nightgown, Kazy knelt in a room warm with firelight and candlelight. There was a fire in the bedchamber, and she could not quite bear to leave it, even for the clean white bed where Beth already lay asleep. It was dark, but much earlier than she had ever gone to bed in Jennet's house. She could not remember when she last felt so safe or so clean—for the hospitality of Collywell Cross even extended to a large tub and buckets of hot water, and clean fresh clothes had been provided for Kazy and Beth.

She had felt safe since the moment the door of Collywell Cross had shut behind her, and gray-haired, gray-clothed Mary Fairlamb had led her, calmly and quietly, into a warm room and drawn them toward the fire while she sent for hot milk and bread. She had not asked anything about who they were or where they came from or how long they wanted to stay. She had waited until Kazy made the next move, and Kazy, remembering what she always thought about Collywell Cross, had not said she was Kate, nor an orphan, nor looking for work. She had looked into Mary's eyes as the rain pelted on the crisscross windows.

"You knew my stepmother, Eliza Clare. This is her daughter, Beth. And I'm Kezia. I'm Kazy Clare."

"Yes, I thought you must be," said Mary simply. "I knew you'd come. Are your feet warm yet?"

All the rooms in Collywell Cross seemed light and airy, with none of the dark paneling and small windows Kazy was accustomed to. The furniture was solid, dark and simple and not much of it, but everywhere was swept and smelled fresh and clean.

"You shall eat with us all tomorrow," Mary had said, "but tonight you shall eat in peace and quiet in your own room." The furniture might be sparse, but the food was plentiful. Kazy found she had forgotten how good Joan's cooking had been, and the stew brought to them was, if anything, better than Joan's. Mary had left them alone to eat it, and when she came back to find them scouring their bowls with bread to get every last taste she had brought them some more. The rain still dashed on the window, but they were safe in their small firelit room, with no one to hide from and no one to lie to. Already, Abbey St. Andrew seemed far away in the past.

Kazy turned at last from the dying firelight to the inviting bed and slipped in beside Beth. She wanted to lie awake, feeling the clean freshness of the linen. As she blew out the candle, footsteps outside stopped at the door.

"Good night, girls, and God bless you," said Mary Fairlamb.

"Good night," said Kazy, and was soon asleep.

The steady ringing of a bell woke them when the dawn was still pale and uncertain. They dressed quickly in the clean clothes they had been given, Eliza's comb was pulled through freshly washed hair, and they opened the door to see everyone else in Collywell Cross steadily making their way outside. Kazy took Beth's hand and followed the crowd along a gallery, down a stair, through arched cloisters around a lawn, and into a chapel. Beyond the chapel was a well, which she supposed must be fed by a spring. Beth, who looked ready to be bored, caught sight of a tabby kitten sitting primly by the chapel door and found it didn't mind at all that she carried it into church with her. Nobody else seemed to mind, either.

Kazy caught her breath as she entered the chapel. The churches she had known before were gray, dark places. Here, the walls were white, and tall beeswax candles added to the light from the cross-paned windows. And flowers! Flowers at the table, flowers at the door, tall and bright with color and smelling fragrant—Kazy was still wondering at all this when a tall man with abundant gray hair and a beard strode in, shouted "Glory to God in the highest!" and began to lead prayers. His face wrinkled when he smiled, which he did most of the time. He seemed to like the word *glory*, saying it as often as he could and as loudly.

A breakfast of bread and wheat porridge followed, in a room with long tables and benches. Mary seated Beth between Kazy and herself, and they were waited on by a young woman with the speech and the air of a gentlewoman—"My daughter, Anne," said Mary. "We all serve each other here."

The big man who had led prayers, and who sat at the other end of the table laughing loudly now and again, was Mary's husband, Hugh. From time to time Mary pointed people out to Kazy—"Anne's husband . . . and their three children . . . and Hugh's old mother"—and there were two very old women and a few children who seemed to be there simply because they had nowhere else to go. Beth's eyes strayed shyly from Mary's face to the little group of children. As the table was cleared, Hugh Fairlamb pronounced a blessing and finished with such a "Glory!" that Beth jumped, blushed, and hid her face against Kazy.

"Hugh, don't shout," said Mary. "You frighten our guests." And she stood up, brushing crumbs from her skirt. "Heigh-ho! There's work to be done."

"Eliza used to say that," said Kazy. There was something of

Eliza, too, in the way Mary smoothed down her gown, and in the way she smiled and held out her hand to Beth. All the smaller children went away with Anne for the morning and Beth, after some coaxing, joined them.

"And you can come with me," said Mary, and led Kazy back toward the chapel. Kazy was ready for some hard questions, but Mary didn't ask her anything. Instead, she talked about Collywell Cross as they walked through the cloisters.

"Long, long ago," she said, "when the first monks came to the North of England, a holy man named Coll came here. This was where he built a cell and a chapel and raised a wooden cross. People came here to be taught, healed, and baptized—especially healed. Some said that Coll had the gift of healing, and some said the water had healing properties. I think it was both. Certainly, it's good water, especially for anyone with stiff old joints. Collywell Cross has always been a healing place.

"Later, when the abbey was built at Abbey St. Andrew, the little chapel here was repaired and they built a sort of guest house and hospital for the abbey. When all the monasteries were closed, Collywell Cross was sold to a friend of the king, who tried to make it more like a house and less like a monastery. But he didn't like it here. The weather was too cold, and there were still raiders living in the hills in those days, who came and helped themselves to the sheep and cattle whenever they wanted to. It was bought and sold, many times, before Hugh and I took it."

Kazy couldn't imagine Mary anywhere else. "Where did you live before that?"

"We had a fine town house in Highbridge. Hugh was a shipper of coal, like his father, and became rich, but he had always wanted to take Holy Orders. There's more to life than money. There are our dreams. Hugh and I dreamed of a house with a chapel, so there would always be prayer and love. Plenty of love, and people to share it with. Then we heard that Collywell Cross was to be sold again, as if it was waiting for us. My daughter and her husband joined us—my son-in-law manages the land. And my son is in Holy Orders and has the parish nearby."

"Who are all the children?"

"Some are our grandchildren, some are the children of people who work here. Some are orphans. They end up here, God bless them. We teach them well and find them apprenticeships when they're old enough, or they might stay and work here. We have more servants than we need, I suppose. But we train them well."

"As you did with Eliza."

Mary stopped walking for a moment and looked into the distance. "Yes," she said. "Eliza was like a daughter to me. You must miss her sorely."

"Nothing has been right since she died," said Kazy. Walking around and around the cloisters with Mary she told everything, starting from when Eliza was alive. She told of Eliza's death, and her own efforts to look after the family, and Aunt Latimer's arrival, and the beatings. She told of her father's refusal to listen, their escape, Willowsford, the tinkers, Thomas Pettigrew, Abbey St. Andrew, Jennet, Beth's illness. Then—Mary heard Kazy's voice drop and watched her hands clenching and stretching against her gown—the overheard conversation in the abbey.

"So," she said, "my mother was known as a clever scold, and my father doesn't want me. And when we ran away I always thought I could bring us all together again. I thought there was something at the heart of our family, something strong and true and good, that would last, like . . . like mother's ring. But I've lost that, too, Mary, I couldn't even keep that. I really didn't think Father would do this to us. Especially to Beth." She bit her lip hard.

"I do wonder," said Mary calmly, "if you can be right about this. Your father has brought your aunt home. That does not mean he has rejected you."

"It does," said Kazy.

"You think it does," said Mary firmly. "I think, my dear, I shall write to your father to let him know that you are here and safe. But I shall ask him to leave you here for a while, in our care. You and Beth need quiet, proper food and rest, before anything else. Is that all right?"

Kazy nodded. It would be safe, nobody would harm them, if Mary wrote for her. She rubbed her eyes so she could see where she was going. Mary took her arm and guided her toward the chapel.

"And will you be happy here?" asked Mary as they seated themselves on a bench in the chapel.

"Oh, yes." She slipped her hand into her pocket, found Eliza's keys, and held them tightly.

"Then why are you crying?" asked Mary, and took her hand.

"Because you're kind . . . because I miss my home . . . and my father . . . and I want Eliza so much . . ." and with her face in Mary's lap, she cried as she had not cried in all the months since Eliza died.

A servant was sent that day with a letter to Cutherham, and another to find Thomas Pettigrew. Kazy had never known the name of his parish, but Mary was concerned about him. In the meantime, Kazy and Beth fell into the pattern of life at Colly-well Cross. Beth was so content to let Kazy out of her sight that Kazy sometimes felt hurt, but there was enough to keep her busy. Everyone at Collywell Cross earned their keep, apart from those who were too young, too old, or ill—one wing of the house was an infirmary, where the sick were cared for. There were prayers three times a day, food to prepare, medicines to be made, rooms to be swept and fruit to be harvested, for the apples, plums, and pears were ripening. But every night she went to bed a little disappointed that her father had not come, and a little relieved.

Hugh laughed heartily at Kazy's attempts to make the bread, and she found the jollity of the Glory Man hard to live with. Jennet and Beth had eaten her bread without complaining. Mary taught her to rock and fold the dough rhythmically, as Eliza did. When Kazy swept a chamber, Mary reminded her to do the corners. It wasn't easy learning again to take orders after working for Jennet, who never cared what the floor was like. But there was enough at Collywell Cross to make Hugh's teasing and the unlearning of bad habits easy to live with. There was music, too. A pair of virginals stood in the hall and Hugh had lent Kazy his lute. She was often asked to play in the evenings, and sometimes she would play outside the infirmary. Most of all, there was Beth, who was safe, cared for, and thoroughly happy. She chattered, laughed, ran around the gardens with the other children, and played with the tabby kitten.

"I'd forgotten that," Kazy said to Mary as they watched from the kitchen door. She was helping Mary with the midday meal, but they had stopped to watch Beth. She was handing the kitten to a small boy with great concern for the safety of both. "She mothers things, as Eliza did. No wonder Father couldn't bear to look at her."

"But you could."

"She's all I have left of Eliza."

"Do you really think so?"

Kazy was puzzled. "Oh, do you mean the keys? But—"

"I mean nothing of the kind. Come and chop the sage leaves, Kazy. I mean the difference that Eliza made to you. Isn't there a bit of Eliza about you?"

Kazy rubbed the pungent leaves from her fingers. "I used to hope so. When she died, I felt that if I couldn't have Eliza, I could be Eliza, at least for Father and Beth. But I can't, because I'm not her, and I'm not like her."

"But you have kindness and loyalty. Do you think that might be something to do with Eliza? Is the sage ready? Stir the pot, please."

Kazy stirred. "How long will it take the messenger to get to Father?" she asked carelessly, as if it didn't matter.

"It depends on the roads, and roads depend on weather,"

said Mary. "Your custard may be done by now. Is your father a very busy man, do you think?"

"Oh, yes," said Kazy, who had forgotten about the custard and was now trying to take it from the oven without burning herself. "The bishop and the—ouch—the other canons consult him all the time. They say nobody else could keep the peace between them all."

"That's very strange," said Mary. "I understood that the canons each have twenty-one days on duty at the cathedral and need to do very little work at other times."

"But he chooses to work hard," said Kazy, "and he has to preach, but not very often. And he's always meeting people and visiting the sick and the poor." Not for the first time, she wished he didn't. "And he tutors young men who are due to go to Oxford."

"Are there many of those in Cutherham?" asked Mary innocently.

"Taste the custard, please," said Kazy. "Is it sweet enough?"

Mary tasted. "It's excellent. I see, so your father can always find plenty to do. What does he not do, Kazy?"

Collywell Cross, thought Kazy. The place where I have to face the truth. She sat down, smoothed her apron, and turned to face Mary.

"He doesn't take notice of Beth and me, I know. But it isn't his fault, Mary. He doesn't really understand much about daughters. He taught me Latin and Greek as if I were a boy, and everyone said it was a waste to educate a girl, but I loved it. But, you see, the only thing he really knows about children is how to teach them. He was just so lost after Eliza died, it was as if he was hiding from us."

"When you ran away, did you mean to hurt him?"

"Oh, no." She looked up into Mary's steady gaze, saw the gray, calm eyes beneath the gray hair. "No!" she said again. Then, "At least, not that much."

Mary said nothing to blame her, but only told her to take off her apron, for she had worked hard enough for the moment. Kazy was about to ask if she could go and play the virginals, when Beth ran in, wet, dirty, and pink with laughter.

"Kazy, come and see, come and see, we've got a—" but she was interrupted by the booming voice of Hugh as he strode in behind her.

"Don't tell her, Beth! Just bring her along! Mary, let her come with us! Glory, what a splendid custard!"

"Don't you dare touch it, Hugh. Go on, Kazy, go with them. There's time enough before prayers and dinner, and I can spare you until then." But Beth already had Kazy's hand in both of hers and was dragging her along. She pulled her all the way past the chapel and the outhouses, down to a shallow stretch of the river. Most of the children were already there with Anne, and Kazy saw what Beth was so excited about.

"We've got a swing! Hugh made a swing!"

A knotted rope hung from a branch of a tree overhanging the river. One of the children, holding on tightly, was swinging back and forth with a grin almost too big for his face. Beth hopped and fidgeted until it was her turn.

"Watch me, watch me!" she cried, as Hugh lifted her to the

rope. Kazy picked up a fir cone from the ground and began nervously to pull it to pieces.

"She'll fall," she whispered.

"She'll have a soft landing, if she does," said Hugh. "Or a wet one. She'll come to no harm." And Beth nearly did fall, when she let go with one hand to wave, but somehow she stayed on.

"Now," shouted Hugh, "Kazy's turn!"

"Not me!" It did look fun, though.

"Yes, Kazy's turn!" cried Beth breathlessly, holding out the rope. "There's nothing to be afraid of."

"Afraid?" Kazy heaved at her gown, took the rope, and jumped, with terror as the rope swung her out of control—exciting, lovely terror, flying out over the water.

"Make it come back!" called Beth, and she found that, with a bit of twisting and pushing, she could make it go more or less where she wanted to. She landed at last at Hugh's feet, stumbling as he caught her.

"Never been on a swing before? Thought not. Try again." This time she swung confidently, leaning back and looking at the sky through the leaves, and not caring when she fell.

It was, as Hugh had said, a soft landing. As she struggled to her feet, she heard his annoying bellow of laughter.

"You could help me up!" Her hem was heavy with damp sand, but Hugh still laughed, and, remembering everything that irritated her about Hugh, she scrabbled for a handful of fir cones and threw them at him. Laughing more heartily than ever he threw them back, and by the time every child had joined in the fir cone fight Kazy was laughing, too, until

Hugh, at last, took her hand and pulled her up the bank. Anne gathered the children together, to get them cleaned and tidied before prayers and Kazy, seeing Anne so motherly and calm, wondered if she had ever thrown fir cones at Hugh when she was a girl. Did families really do things like that? Perhaps she had forgotten what being a child was like.

By the time she had tidied herself up, she had to hurry for chapel. She ran all the way and looked for an empty place near the back. There, she recognized the gaunt, shabby figure of Thomas Pettigrew.

She heard nothing of the service. All she could see in her head were the gray face of Grace Pettigrew, and her own pearl earrings on the table.

When prayers were over, she stayed until the others had left. Thomas Pettigrew stayed, too, with his head bowed in prayer, but when at last he looked up and saw her, a brightness came into his face.

"Canon Clare's daughter!" he said, and she realized how useless her earrings had been, because, of course, he would not have sold them. "I have prayed for you. I was most concerned."

"I'm sorry," she faltered. But he seemed not to notice.

"Your father has been so kind, very kind. A messenger from Cutherham brought him to me, and he was most concerned about us. He provided sea coal and firewood and food, he even paid for a physician. My poor Grace is dead—but she died in good care. Then Mistress Fairlamb invited me here—everyone is kind. But my poor Grace . . ." he rubbed at his eyes, which looked pink-rimmed and swollen.

"I'm so sorry," she said again, and, to show she understood, added, "my stepmother died, too. But this has always been a healing place." She took his hand and led him to the hall for dinner.

The next day started badly. She slept late, ran in late to chapel, where she had a coughing fit, and spilled hot water on her hand in the kitchen. Then it was her turn in the infirmary to help with the feeding of those patients who could not feed themselves, and an old man who smelled unpleasant took a little porridge and was sick. When Mary took her to one side and led her to the chapel after dinner she wondered what other mistakes she had made, but Mary was as calm as ever, and seated her on a bench.

"I have word from Cutherham," she said. Kazy felt hot, then cold, and her strength drained. But nothing could be worse than being disowned.

"What does he say?"

"He sends his great love and care for you both. He desires to come to you as soon as I think it good. He is happy for you to stay here at present."

"But does he want us back?"

"Of course he wants you back! Here. Read it yourself."

Her father's hand, so strange in that place, made Collywell Cross seem like his chamber in Cutherham. It was a long letter, but there were phrases that stood out:

". . . inquiries were made everywhere by a Master Challoner, sent by my sister-in-law, Mistress Katherine Lawrence of York . . ."

"Oh," said Kazy. "So that man was from Aunt Lawrence, not Aunt Latimer. If only I'd known." She read on:

". . . my sister, Frances, had been acting most strangely, and even burned a letter from Kazy before it could reach me. After this we could agree on nothing, and she left my house and went to some relations of her late husband—but she became ill of a seizure, which left her withered, with no movement on one side of her body and almost no speech, and needing more care than they could give her, so I brought her back to my home."

"If only I'd known that, too," said Kazy as she put the letter down. "Isn't everything a tangle?"

"One thing is clear, tangle or no tangle," said Mary. "Your father cares about you."

"He cares." She took a minute to let this sink in and warm her. "But there's still a tangle. It's a tangle of terrible things that happen, and I shouldn't say this, but God lets them happen. He let Eliza and Grace Pettigrew become ill and die. He lets little children like Beth fall into the hands of people like my aunt. He lets people turn witless, like Jennet. Why? That's a tangle."

Mary appeared to be looking at the flowers in the chapel. Then she said, "How does your recorder work?"

"You cover the holes," said Kazy without interest. "So the sound comes out at different points with different pitch."

"And how does that work?"

"Something to do with how hard you blow. The amount of air and how it moves. Oh, I don't know. Do you?"

"No, my dear, and I think if neither of us can understand a

recorder we really can't expect to understand God. All I know is this. At the heart of everything, there is something that Eliza brought to your home, there is something that made you rescue Beth, something that makes your father miss you so much. Something at the heart of Collywell Cross. There is love, Kazy, in the tangle and beyond it. Love. And that's all we can really know. But," she finished, standing up and straightening the flowers in their stone jars, "if you don't believe me, you can always complain to God. He's strong enough to stand it."

Kazy did not feel like complaining to God just then. The relief of knowing that her father forgave her was enough, and she was, as usual, kept busy. Collecting wood was a favorite task—all the children helped, because they could take turns riding on the little hand-pulled cart and falling off. But a day came when Beth asked so often when Father would be coming that Kazy was sure she was doing it on purpose to be annoying. It was what Mary called a "spilled milk" day, when everyone seemed out of temper, and the weather was sullen, and so was the fire in the hearth, and, in the evening, Kazy's fingers seemed too clumsy to play a true note, and Hugh grinned at her mistakes. Out of temper with everything and everyone, she walked in the twilight to Colly's Well and the chapel. The chapel was always peaceful, lit by the tall beeswax candles.

She thought of Thomas Pettigrew, grieving for his wife who had suffered such pain and poverty, and the world was full of pain and poverty. She thought of her father, who had seen the two bright loves of his life die young. Motherless, ill-treated Beth.

"Just tell me why, God," she whispered. "Why? If you're so

powerful, why do you allow it all? I'm going to stay here until you tell me."

It grew darker and cooler, and she stayed. Nothing happened. Of course, she thought, of course God won't answer me. Why should he? He doesn't have to. And what is the point of arguing with someone who won't argue back?

She remembered Mary's words: "If we can't understand how a recorder works, how can we understand God?" Mary had said something else, too.

Kazy stood up, wrapping her arms around herself for warmth. Behind the windows the sky grew streaky with twilight, and inside the chapel the candles wore haloes in the soft darkness. She looked steadily at the gentle candle flames and at the long creamy ribbons growing as the molten wax gathered and ran down the columns. Beeswax scented the air with honey. And even though she still had no answers, she found she no longer could be angry or resentful. Something in the chapel was so powerful that she was afraid and, at the same time, so lovely, that it was safe to be afraid.

"There is always love. Always, in the tangle and beyond it."

In the chapel at Collywell Cross there were no answers, only love.

Kazy had no idea how long she stayed there. When she left, the first star of the evening was above her.

Nothing could annoy her the next day, not even Hugh. When he asked her to play the lute for the patients in the infirmary she agreed willingly, and, after dinner, took her place near the open door, playing and singing. There was the usual coming and going of different people walking past, and fragments of conversation drifted by her. Then two voices drew nearer, growing louder and stronger. One of them was Hugh's, too loud to be ignored, and the sound of her own name caught her attention, so that she played a wrong note. What he said next made her stop playing altogether.

". . . I know it wasn't a wise thing, but what else could Kazy do? Wait until you came to your senses? She tried, Clare. You tell me you had always been in awe of your sister, so didn't you want to rescue your daughters from her?"

"Frances had always seemed to be right."

At the sound of her father's voice, Kazy clutched the neck of the lute very tightly. She slipped the other hand to her mouth and bit her knuckle.

"Right, Clare? Right? I doubt the scars will ever go, and you call it right? If you weren't so wrapped up in your own grief, you would have stood up to your sister!"

"I have no defense but only hope. Hope in God, in Kazy, and in Collywell Cross."

"It won't do, Clare! God, Kazy, and Collywell Cross? What about yourself, man? What about making some changes there?"

Fight him, Father, thought Kazy. Stand up to him.

"I have thought long about that," said Walter Clare.

"Thought? Thought? It's not enough, Clare, not enough! What do you intend to do about it?"

She would not wait for any more. Already she had taken her gown in both hands and was running from the doorway.

"Stop this at once, Hugh! Leave him alone!"

But the sight of her father made her forget what she was saying. He looked so much more real and older than in all her rememberings, and at the same time so bewildered, like a lost child. As he saw her, his face took on such pain and intensity that she was afraid—would he cry, would he hit her? But, above all, she saw that he needed her.

"It's all right," she said, and held out her hands to him. "We're safe here. We can start again." And she took him to the chapel while Hugh, for once, laughed quietly and walked away.

Kazy and her father sat for a long time with their arms around each other, and both cried a little, and both said sorry to each other, because they both knew how much they had to be sorry about. It was enough, for the moment, just to be together. Then a child ran past the window and he looked up sharply, and Kazy knew who he was looking for. She took his arm and together they walked down to the river, where, long before they saw anyone, they heard the shrieks and laughter of the children playing on the swing.

It was Beth's turn on the rope and, seeing only Kazy, she waved and fell off. She was not hurt, and only a little wet, and splashed water at Kazy, who was laughing at her—then she stood still, and stared as if she had seen something too wonderful to believe, and so she wouldn't believe it. She looked from her father to Kazy, and Kazy realized at that moment how long it was since Beth had seen him. Canon Clare saw the laughing child in the water and wondered what had happened to the staring, stammering shadow of the Cutherham house.

"Yes, Beth," said Kazy. "It really is Father." And Beth, in a wild, wet rush, was in her father's arms and pulling him away to the garden to see the kitten. Kazy followed behind them, wondering if she were needed, and remembering what Mary had said about love.

At evening chapel, Beth fell asleep in her father's arms, and she stayed there, still asleep, in the twilight as Canon Clare and Kazy walked around and around the sweet-smelling gardens. They had talked all day, but there was something else to ask.

"How is my aunt?"

"I was coming to that. You know that she had a seizure? I should have realized this would come—she was always complaining of headaches, always angry as if the blood in her veins was ready to boil over. I suppose, Kazy, I was as careless of her as I was of you. Now she cannot walk, nor do anything for herself. She is back, Kazy. Joan manages as best she can. However long my sister has to live, and it may be very long, there will be no improvement."

She felt she ought to say she was sorry to hear it, but she couldn't. He told her of all his journeys to York and Highbridge, and of Challoner, Mistress Lawrence's man, who had sought them so long. ". . . and thought he had you, too, until you gave the tinkers the slip. We traced the tinkers after a distinctive set of pearls was seen to be offered for sale by a disreputable jeweler for a fraction of its true worth."

"Don't make trouble for the tinkers, Father. They don't mean any harm."

"And Pettigrew," he said grimly, then was silent for so long that Kazy thought he was angry.

"I had no idea," he said at last, "that any of our clergy lived so poor, until he stood before me with your earrings in his hands and hunger in his face. He had sold the few books and the little silver he had to pay the physician. If I had known, Kazy, if I had known about them, and if I had known about *this*!" He gazed about Collywell Cross, where lights glowed softly from the infirmary. "She could have come here, they would have been helped . . . and Eliza talked so often of Collywell Cross, while I pretended to listen. Well, Kazy, I will make sure of a better income for Master Pettigrew. Challoner traced you to Abbey St. Andrew, and I was ready to go there if Mistress Fairlamb's message had not reached me."

Beth wriggled and slowly woke up. Kazy reached out to her, but Beth pushed her away.

"Kezia, Kezia, your house is on fire," she muttered, and fell asleep again.

"I wish she wouldn't say that," said Kazy with a shudder. "I don't mind the silly rhyming. I just don't like hearing about . . ." it was hard to say, and she said it quietly, "houses on fire."

Then, realizing that he hadn't known about that, she told him about Jennet and the fire and Will.

"And no one is to be angry with Will for helping us to hide," she said. "He did all he could to help us. I wouldn't have brought Beth here, if not for Will. He's kind all the way through. When the fire happened, he—oh!" There was a sharp pain of memory. "Father, I'm so sorry!" And she told him about the wedding ring, and how it had been lost in the fire.

"Well," he said, "you are safe. And Beth."

The bell rang for supper, and she led him to the refectory, where the great fire crackling in the hearth made them realize how cold it had become outside and a firelit glow burnished the dark table. Kazy took Beth from her father's arms and woke her gently. This, she thought, is as it should be. Beth, Father, and me, at a warm fireside at suppertime. Of course, Eliza should be here. But we are learning to live without Eliza.

Nothing can be rushed at Collywell Cross, thought Kazy, as day after day she saw its healing at work in her father, as it worked in Thomas Pettigrew. But already Beth was asking when they would go home, and, at last, Kazy knew she had to ask. She raised the subject after breakfast one morning as they walked down to Colly's Well.

"Father, when do we go home?"

"Do you want to go home?" Then, seeing that his answer had shaken her, he sat her down beside the well. "Of course I want you home! But do you realize what that means? You would need to take charge of the housekeeping, the stores, the linen, the money, the clothes—of course, Joan will be there, as always. But it is a hard thing for a girl of thirteen, who should be enjoying her music and reading, and choosing new lace collars and cuffs."

"But shall I still have my lessons and my music?"

"Of course you can, Kazy, but think how much else will be asked of you! You will need to care for Beth and for your aunt, who is as helpless as a little child, though her mind is sharp. Could you do all that?"

"Do I have a choice?"

"Your Aunt Lawrence in York would gladly give you a home. And Beth. In the past, she offered to care for you, and I refused, because I wanted to keep you. Perhaps it would have been better for you if I had agreed. She would be good to you both, Kazy. She could offer you a fuller life than I can, in a big, fashionable house where you could meet the wise and the wealthy—and you could come to see me, now and again. Or—and I have talked of this to the Fairlambs—there is Collywell Cross."

"I love Collywell Cross," she said.

"I hope we will all come back here many times. It has drawn us all to itself. If you wish to stay here, and share with the Fairlambs in the work of Collywell Cross, you may. Beth can make her own choice, but I think she will be happy wherever you are."

"She needs us both."

"I would come to visit you frequently, my dear. Tomorrow, I must go to Abbey St. Andrew. I have business there, and I wish to meet the valiant Will Sheppard."

"Tell him we're safe. And don't get him into trouble for helping us."

"Trouble? I wish to speak with Master Norris about some work to be done at Cutherham Cathedral. The decision is yours, my dear. York . . ."

"No."

". . . Cutherham, or Collywell Cross. I will not force you."

In the afternoon she sat in the branches of a pear tree, hearing the shush and rustle of the wind in the topmost leaves, and turning Eliza's keys over in her hands. When all the fruit worth picking had been taken to the house she had stayed there, rocking a little, looking over at Collywell Cross. She could see Beth in the kitchen garden, helping to dig up carrots and showing off how big they were. Mary went to and fro with baskets of laundry. Somewhere in that square of buildings herbs were mixed into salves, wheat was worked into bread, pain was eased and prayer was offered. Eliza had helped in these gardens and prayed in this chapel. Perhaps, thought Kazy, she prayed for me. Something of me will always belong here, where I learned again to be a child, and to cry, and to grow up. Beth is happy here, with other children and kittens and places to play.

Wherever I go, Beth will go. It would be cruel to expect her to choose between me and Father when she needs us both. Father needs us, too, so I have to keep us together, and that means Cutherham.

But wouldn't Beth love York, and all it could offer her? I

wouldn't, but Beth would. Or she would be happy here, if Father visited us often. He says he will.

And I couldn't run the house. I have so much still to learn. I barely managed at Jennet's house, and she didn't expect much. I can't even take good care of Beth. I nearly let her drink bad water. I nearly got us arrested for witchcraft. She fell ill, she disappeared with Jennet, she was in a house fire, all when she was in my care. That day when Jennet took her away was the worst, and when they were home, I'd been so frightened, I nearly hit her. I've been impatient with her, too. I've expected her to put up with so much, and she's only six. Perhaps I'm no better than Aunt Latimer.

There was Aunt Latimer to consider, too. Kazy put her arm around a branch of the tree and stroked it.

I came to Collywell Cross to face the truth. I have to go away now, because I haven't faced all the truth yet. I have to face Aunt Latimer and forgive her, even if she hasn't forgiven me. If I can't forgive her I will wither and grow sour and become like her.

She knew, now, what to say to her father. There was something else to mention, too, and she rehearsed the way she would say it. She would say, "Father, I'm sorry if this hurts you, but Kazy is a child's name, a baby name. And it's a way of not talking about my mother. I want to know about her. And I want to take my own name. She gave it to me, with a gold ring and my life, and I want to claim it. I am Kezia."

There were a few last things she had to do, and she climbed

down and made her way to the river. She must ask Mary about the tabby kitten. And it would not be possible for the lady of a canon's house to play on a rope swing, so she must make the most of her opportunity.

In the Cutherham streets there was something to talk about for days to come, and the delightful thing was that it was different on every street corner. Everybody had their own story of Canon Clare's daughters. Some said they had been visiting the rector of Abbey St. Andrew, and some that they had been banished from their home. Some said they had run away with the Gypsies, and some that they had been ordered out by That Mistress Latimer and sent to work on a farm at Willowsford. Some said young Kezia Clare was an arrogant little piece who should never be allowed in her father's house again, or that at least she should be whipped and dragged through the streets, and others said she had saved an old woman from a fire and was famous for it in Abbey St. Andrew—then they stopped talking, as they heard the approach of horses' hooves, and they all decided that if the young madam had any reason to be ashamed of herself, she didn't look like it.

Was that really young Kezia Clare, riding straight-backed beside her father? Wherever she had been, she had grown up. What had happened to give her that calm, decided look? And there was the pretty one, too, all curls and dimples in the saddle in front of Canon Clare, looking just like her mother. And you know what they say. They say Kezia is just like her mother, too, and more's the pity.

She had forgotten how dark the Cutherham house was, after Collywell Cross, but there was the old hearth, and the paneling with the same old scratches on it, and the rushlight holder that was never quite straight, and Joan! Joan, hurrying from the kitchen with both hands held out and tears in her eyes—"My girls, my lovely girls!"—and wrapping them both in her arms, and telling them with sobs that she had baked all the things they loved—there was a warm, spicy fragrance from the kitchen. They were home.

Canon Clare looked about him, then looked at Joan. "Is she . . .?"

"She's abed, sir. I thought I'd not bring her down, sir, just yet."

"Quite right. We shall go up shortly. Take Beth to the kitchen, before the fragrance of gingerbread overcomes her. And as you will see, Joan, we have acquired a kitchen cat."

When they had gone, he reached into his coat pocket. He took out something very small, wrapped in a cloth.

"This is yours, Kezia," he said.

Kazy unwrapped it and took a deep, slow breath. The gold ring gleamed in her palm, and it was perfect.

"It can't be," she said. "It was in the fire."

"That day I went to Abbey St. Andrew," he said, "Will and I looked for it in the rubble at Jennet's house. I knew we would find it. This is pure gold. Tested by fire, but not destroyed. Kezia, you are your mother's daughter!"

"Don't," she said. "You'll make me cry."

In the room where she had crawled in her nightgown to steal the birch rod, Kazy stood and surveyed the figure in the bed.

The tyrant who had beaten and scared and deprived them was a slumped figure, half propped on a pillow, dribbling a little.

The old woman in her nightgown and cap regarded her with a puzzled, lopsided look. She reminded Kazy of Jennet, but without Jennet's energy. This one would not wander about in the night. She shuffled a little, but was helpless to do much. If you could, wondered Kazy, would you still beat Beth? Do you know who I am? Do you want to beat me? But it mattered not at all. It was a startling fact, but it was so. It didn't matter.

She bent over the bed and eased the sliding figure more comfortably against the pillows. A childish watchfulness came into Aunt Latimer's eyes, the way Beth used to look when she was afraid. Kazy saw what it meant to Aunt Latimer to be helpless, and with all her heart felt sorry for her.

"There, now," she said. "I won't hurt you." She lifted a corner of the sheet and, very gently, wiped the thin line of dribble from the wrinkled chin.